Crown of the Exiled

CROWN

OF THE

EXILED

A CROWN OF THE PHOENIX NOVEL

C. A. VARIAN

INAS

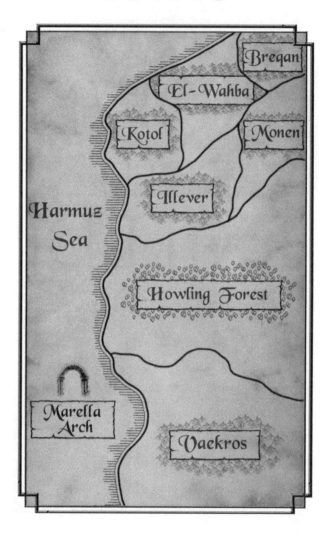

EKOTORIA

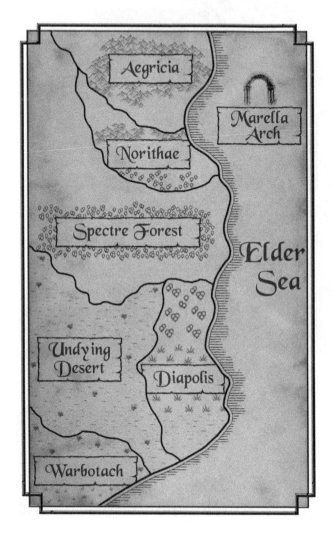

Aurelia and Cristos

Exie and Septima

Contents

Chapter 1

Aurelia

The last words Aurelia Vesta wanted to hear when the chaos of battle settled and the enemy retreated into the forest was that her sister, Septima, the person she'd left her world for, was gone.

She knew there was a chance they all wouldn't make it back alive when they'd left the safety of their camp and traveled into Warbotach-controlled Norithae that morning. It was what had caused near constant fear in Aurelia's chest ever since Blaedia had planned the siege days earlier, but she never expected the enemy to take her sister.

Their decision to leave the human world only months prior had been the biggest decision of their lives, and albeit ill-planned, had been the right decision. They had been through so much already, so much bad, yet so much good. They'd spent time in a dungeon, had been attacked by hellhounds, but they'd also found love. Even traveling into a fae realm that was on the brink of war, and even after their father, Proteus, had ignored the fact that Septima was not attracted to males and had arranged their marriages anyway, they'd found love.

Aurelia and Septima had run away from home, deciding any destiny was better than the one their father had made for them, but they'd never anticipated running into fae warriors in the forest of the human realm. They'd never even known another realm existed. The portal was so close to their home, but they could've never traversed it on their own. The Aegrician phoenix warriors were the only beings in either world with the ability to fly through the Marella Arch and travel between the worlds, although leaders of both realms had decided long ago that the portal should remain unused to prevent exactly what threatened the two realms now—war.

Barbarians from the magical realm had been attempting to take over the human world for months, wanting to move to the fertile land on the other side since their own was dying with the spread of the desert on the southern part of the continent. No one knew why the Warbotach ruler hadn't stopped after his conquest of the northern kingdoms of

Norithae and Aegrician but was instead desperate to continue his invasion beyond the realm, and no one knew who was backing him. The possibilities of those on other continents backing the king, and the powers they could potentially have, were endless, and they were terrifying.

Having conquered their way across the continent, the Warbotach king had the Aegrician queen, Otera, locked away in her own dungeon. Aurelia had only just discovered her own relation to the Aegrician queen weeks earlier. Otera was her aunt, her mother's sister, and she may never have the chance to meet her. Uldon, the barbarian king, intended to keep Otera locked away until she agreed to give her power to cross the portal, the power of her crown, to him and Aurelia didn't even know if it was possible for the queen to force the crown's power on another. The Crown of the Phoenix had always chosen the queen and who would control the portal between realms, but Uldon clearly believed there was a way for him to take that power. Otera had been held in the dungeon beneath her castle for the past several months as he tried to force her hand.

In the meantime, the Aegrician military, which consisted of phoenix-shifting females and the non-shifting members who worked with them, spent those months away from their kingdom, building up strength and trying to secure allies. If they had not fled, they would have been exterminated. To keep the military and the kingdom's civilians safe, the queen and her leadership agreed on a plan to look for allies and bide their time until they understood what they were up against and were strong enough to win.

Until the previous morning when they'd left their camp in the Spectre Forest and marched toward Norithae, Aurelia and Septima had been to Norithae only once before. Having been captured by Warbotach soldiers while on a hunt, they'd spent time in the dungeon there until the Norithae king, Cristos, had helped them escape. At the time, no one knew Cristos' identity. After the Warbotach cavalry had killed his father, leaving him the new king, Cristos had hidden who he was until he could do the same thing the Aegricians were trying to do---build up allies to take his kingdom back.

In the time since he'd helped them escape the dungeon, he and Aurelia had fallen in love. They had been through so much together, and now they stood in the forest, among the dead and the injured. Their own bodies were bruised and bleeding, but all that mattered in that moment was the devastating words coming from Exie. *Septima is gone.*

Aurelia's heart pounded in her chest, her own bleeding arm no match for her emotions. She had to find her sister.

Exie stood in front of her and Cristos, the blond warrior leaning to one side as her leg gushed blood from a wound in her thigh.

"We have to go after her," she said, her voice full of desperation.

Trying to focus her attention on her friend, the adrenaline surging through Aurelia's body made it difficult. Her eyes scanned the surrounding forest, searching the faces of the warriors who'd shifted back into their fae forms and were now trying to assess who needed a healer and who couldn't be saved. Septima's beautiful tawny face and long obsidian braids were not among them.

"We're going to find her, Exie," she said as she pulled the injured female into her arms. "We're going to find her, but you need to see a healer. You can't fight any more like this."

The warrior's head was shaking before Aurelia had even finished getting the words out. Exie had been injured in battle countless times before, but she'd never let it stop her, and she surely didn't intend to let it keep her from finding the woman she loved.

Just as Exie was about to respond, the tall silver-haired warrior, Holera, and her muscular male lover, Kason, darted out through the trees, bloody but not showing any obvious wounds.

"What's going on?"

Having been Exie's friend since they were young, Holera approached her friend first and looked her over, trying to assess the wound on her leg.

Face appearing grim, Cristos' eyebrows furrowed as he held onto Aurelia's hand. His touch grounded her. "Warbotach took Septima. We can't find her anywhere. She's not among the injured." Exie crumbled, dropping to her knees and sobbing in her hands, completely ignoring her own injury.

"We have to find her,"

Exie said again, the words muffled through her fingers.

"You're wasting time! Go after her now or I'll go myself!"

Lowering herself to the ground, Holera tried to slow the bleeding.

"We're going to find her but you're not going anywhere but to a healer, Exie."

Holera turned to a passing healer, one whose name Aurelia did not know, and called out to her.

"You there, take Exie to the infirmary tent. Advise Blaedia that Septima has been taken and we're going after her. Look after Exie with your life. I want a full report on her when I return."

Cristos pulled Aurelia into his arms, his leathery black wings beating with a panicked urgency as he lifted them through the trees of Spectre Forest and into the sky. She ignored the injury to her arm, the sting of it barely noticeable against the painful wrenching of her chest. Being able to sense her emotions, Cristos kissed her on the cheek as they moved below the setting sun.

"Don't worry, Aurelia. We're going to find her."

Holding her bow at the ready and scanning the forest, Aurelia wasn't so sure. Holera and Kason flew beside them, Holera in her phoenix form while Kason sat astride her back, his own bow ready to strike.

The Warbotach cavalry had snuck up on their ranks as they'd moved toward Norithae to retake the kingdom. They'd been able to sneak up on such trained fighters by using wards that made them invisible, the same type the Aegricians used to camouflage their camps. If Septima was under those wards now, they wouldn't be able to find her. As they searched from the sky, Aurelia was worried that was the case. She could have been right under their nose and they wouldn't have seen her. They wouldn't even have been able to hear her.

They flew for hours, doing low sweeps over the forest and into the mountain pass, but Septima and the Warbotach warriors were gone, or they were hiding behind wards that cloaked their location. Either way, they would not find her on this night.

Aurelia sobbed against Cristos' chest as they made their way back to the location of their camp. They couldn't have gone any further, not without the full might of the military. Aegricia was a Warbotach stronghold. If her sister had been taken there, they would be powerless to get her back, not unless the Diapolisian king decided to provide aid, not unless there was a plan.

Just as they crossed into their own warded space, the temporary camp that had been set up only the night before, Aurelia saw the injured Exie sitting on a bench near the perimeter, her thigh wrapped in bandages. Returning to the camp without Septima in tow was soul-shattering enough, but the look on the blond warrior's face threatened to fracture Aurelia's heart completely. There was no doubt Exie would have gone after Septima if she could have. The fierce warrior had never backed down from a fight, but the injury to her thigh had rendered her nearly immobile.

"I'm going to find Blaedia and update her," Holera said before walking off, Kason following closely behind.

Aurelia had not seen the general since before they'd left for the battle that morning, not since Blaedia made the powerful speech that had every one of the warriors willing to die in battle. With the battle in Norithae being over, it would only be a matter of time before their camp was packed up again and moved into the capital city of Windreach, where Cristos would take his place on the Norithaean throne.

The betrayal still stung, but Aurelia understood why Cristos had not revealed his true identity as heir to the slain king. She may have understood, but she still didn't know how she felt about who he truly was, no matter how much she loved him. He wanted her to be his queen, but the thought of being the human queen of a fae kingdom (technically half-human after what she'd learned from the healer, Variel) was more than she could process, especially with her sister being missing. For the time being, she and Cristos loved each other, and they were together, but the future was still unknown. Being queen, the cryptic Aegrician prophecy, her mother's true identity... It was all too much to process, so Aurelia pushed the heavy thoughts to the back of her mind and turned her attention to Exie, who was still sitting on the bench.

"What happened?" The warrior shifted uncomfortably, her eyes squeezing shut before opening wide. "Was there no trace of her?"

Rubbing a hand over his inky black hair, Cristos shook his head as Aurelia lowered herself onto the bench next to her friend, taking Exie by the hand. With her hands already trembling, she realized she was holding Exie's hand just as much to console herself.

"There was no trace of her or of Warbotach."

Exie blew out a deep breath, her face crumpling.

"I should have gone after her."

"There's nothing you could have done, Exie."

Crouching in front of them, Cristos' features were soft.

"They must have hidden themselves behind wards, just like they did before they attacked us. I don't know how they are summoning the power to keep the wards up, but there's no other explanation."

"We have to find her. She's strong, but we can't leave her in Warbotach hands. If they realized who you are, Aurelia, if they realize her sister is Queen Otera's niece..."

She hesitated, her head moving in a slow shake.

"There's no limit to what they would do to Septima to get to you or to get to the queen."

Aurelia's stomach tightened into a knot, bile burning the back of her throat. She hadn't had time yet to realize what it would mean for Septima if Warbotach found out her connection to the queen who was locked away in her own dungeon. When she stood onto shaky legs, the burden on Aurelia's shoulders made them almost too heavy to carry. She swayed, Cristos swooping in and wrapping an arm around her waist before turning her toward their tent.

"We all need to get some sleep," he said as he held onto her. "There's nothing we can do right now, but we will find her. I promise you. We will find her."

When they walked away, Aurelia hesitant to leave her friend at all, Exie was still sitting on the bench with her face in her hands.

Chapter 2

Septima

Septima's silken braids swung wildly below her as she lay unconscious astride the saddle of a Warbotach warrior's horse. The monstrous rider dug his heels into his crimson mount, traveling swiftly under the cover of Spectre Forest, taking Aurelia's sister toward the kingdom of Aegricia and further from the only family she had in the fae realm.

The turbulence of the ride jolted her awake, but only for a moment, not long enough for her to realize what was happening to her. When she awoke again, untold hours later, the crackling of a fire warmed her skin, but the bindings that bit into her wrists burned more than the flames. She struggled, twisting in her spot on the leaf-littered forest floor, but it was no use. Her vision was still blurry as she opened her eyes, trying to make sense of the darkness, of the chaotic surroundings where nothing looked familiar. There was no

Aurelia, no Exie, not even the colorful flap of fiery wings. She tried to stand, but ropes held her ankles tight, so she only fell to the ground again.

"Stop struggling."

The unfamiliar voice came from somewhere behind her. It was deep and gravelly. *Not a friend.*

Twisting to face him, the sight of the scar faced Warbotach male pulled a scream from her gagged mouth. She scurried back on the ground, coming to a halt only feet away from the stones surrounding the fire.

"You're not getting away, female. So, stop struggling."

With only flickers of memory, she didn't even know how she'd gotten there. Her head pounded, sending her vision spinning as she scanned her surroundings again. From what she could tell, she was still in Spectre Forest. Realizing she was alone in the forest with a lone Warbotach soldier, Septima's skin prickled, fear blooming from her chest and spreading across her body. She didn't know why he'd stolen her, or what he planned to do with her, but she'd never been so unsure of her safety. Not even when she and her sister had been locked away in the Norithaean dungeon had she been so afraid.

Thinking about her time in captivity brought back an ache in her heart, just thinking about Exie being tortured, just thinking about how out of her mind with worry her lover must be with her disappearance. And her sister—she couldn't even think about how worried Aurelia probably was. They were undoubtedly searching the forest for her, if they'd even made it. With the violence of the battle she'd been taken from, she didn't even know if they'd survived. It was tearing her apart. She needed to get away from her captor and find her family and friends.

Even though she was a human in a magical world, and had only been there for mere months, she and her sister had found a new family, a new group of friends who would do anything to keep them safe. She'd found love, a love like she could have never had back in her home world where women were not allowed to marry other women. Exie was everything she'd ever wanted in a partner, and she knew her lover felt the same way. She knew Exie would tear down the world to find her, because she was strong and courageous, and the passion and love they felt for each other was real.

The male's dark eyes watched her as though she were an insect he needed to swat, but she broke the stare, scooting on the ground until she faced the fire, leaving her back to him. It wasn't until she turned around, and gazed across the fire, that she saw them. *All of them.*

Chapter 3

Otera

The days seemed to drag on since the last time Uldon had visited Otera's cell in the dungeon. She wasn't complaining. He was the last person she wanted to see. The face she really wanted to see, although it wasn't her true face at all, was Bremusa. Her friend, the elemental hiding in plain sight, had not been to her cell since she'd cleaned the queen's wounds. Otera wasn't sure how long it had been since she'd enraged the Warbotach king enough for him to strike her, but she didn't regret a thing. He was getting desperate. After everything he'd already tried to bend her crown to his will so he could get through the portal and into the human world, he'd been unsuccessful. All it did was show how unhinged Uldon really was. The queen smirked as she traced her fingers along the new scar beneath her eye, the wound having healed quickly due to her fae blood.

With only the sliver of a window to let in a view of the sun and moon, she'd lost track of the days as they passed, each one blending into the next. She wasn't sure how long she'd been in the dungeon, and with no visits from Uldon to brag about his attempts to steal her power, she truly had no concept of time at all. So Otera sat in silence, a small flame dancing in the palm of her hand and waited for the sun to rise again and mark another day she would lose track of as she served as a prisoner in her own palace.

The silence was maddening, giving her too much time to think. Until she'd been told about the capture of her commander and several of her warriors, Otera had been strong. She'd done her best to steal her mind and not think about those she loved more than anything, but as time went on with nothing to fill her days, no kingdom to rule, she began to grieve, began to feel a pit growing in her stomach that made it difficult to eat the meager meals they left for her on the dungeon floor. She knew she'd lost weight, knew her ribs had never been as pronounced as they now were. The urge to eat slowed just as the updates on her people had.

At the beginning of her imprisonment, the ravens came regularly, their messages passed on through Bremusa. It didn't take long for the ravens to stop coming though, or at least the messages to stop coming to her. Bremusa no longer brought her daily meals. Instead, Uldon's sniveling, cowardly advisor brought them. He was too afraid of Otera to come alone, so he never entered the dungeon without at least one of the beastly, scarred warriors that filled the Warbotach ranks, which filled her with a delirious giddiness. In her shredded dress and filthy skin, she was certainly not as fierce as she'd been before being pulled from her bed in the middle of the night, so being able to intimidate at least one person felt like a victory. In her pathetic existence, it was the small victories that counted.

Chapter 4

Aurelia

There was a somber mood in the Aegrician war camp as Aurelia and Cristos made their way toward Kano's enclosure. The great tiger was always situated beside their tent, something Aurelia was grateful for. After the battle, she knew the lanistas had taken him back to camp while she'd looked for Septima. She knew he was at least unharmed after he'd ferociously defended her in battle. With her sister being gone, she needed to see him, if only to cuddle him for a few moments.

Cristos' muscular arm was still wrapped around Aurelia's waist as she walked, if only to hold her upright when all her legs wanted to do was collapse. She was exhausted and over-whelmed. With the disappearance of Septima, she'd almost forgotten about the battle that morning, about how she'd killed people that day. Even knowing she had no other choice, it wasn't something she could just brush off, and she knew she would see their faces when she slept. The tinge of pain shot through her arm as they walked, the injury she had completely forgotten about had clotted but still needed to be cleaned and bandaged. The realization barely had a chance to brush past her mind before the commanding presence of the general approached from outside her tent.

Blaedia walked with a purpose, stopping in front of Aurelia and pulling her into an embrace. Aurelia froze in place, the sudden show of emotion unexpected. Nothing about the general spoke of her being one who would do such a thing.

"We'll find her, Aurelia."

Loosening a breath, Aurelia leaned into Blaedia as the female passed a hand along her back. Her tears had dried up, but the backs of her eyes still burned, the general's embrace only tugging at her frazzled emotions that much more.

"I have no doubt they're bringing her to Aegricia. If so, she'll be with Queen Otera. Our queen won't let anything happen to her. This I can promise you."

When Blaedia pulled away to look into her eyes, the general's face was visibly pained in a way Aurelia had never seen. She didn't know how many warriors they'd lost in the day's battle, but she couldn't imagine how it affected Blaedia when she'd led warriors to their deaths, no matter the reason.

Aurelia nodded, unsure how to respond. No one could make any guarantees about her sister, not even such a powerful warrior.

"Will we be heading to Norithae soon?"

Knowing taking back the city would bring with it another set of complications, she had to bite back her hesitation to ask. Complicated or not, they needed to move closer to Aegricia, closer to where the enemy would be taking her sister. If they couldn't reclaim Norithae, they would never be able to take back Aegricia, and that was their reason for doing everything. All of it was for Aegricia.

Blaedia glanced toward Cristos, the new king of Norithae, her face expectant as though she were waiting for him to speak. It still caught Aurelia by surprise to think about the male who'd been her lover for months being a king. She swallowed back her conflicted emotions while looking at his handsome face, tan skin, and bright cerulean eyes. His black hair was a bit longer than it had been when he'd broken her out of the dungeon, making him look even sexier. The massive leathery wings that framed his back still blew her away. He looked like a god, even with his torn, blood-covered fighting leathers. Glancing down at her own clothing, she realized they both needed a shower and something clean to wear.

Cristos ran his fingers through his hair before he looked up at Blaedia, his brow furrowed.

"We didn't fly over the capital. I didn't want to alert Warbotach if they were still there, but the pass was clear. Well, unless they were under wards, which is possible."

Blaedia nodded but let him continue.

"Still, we need to take back the city, if only to get us closer to Aegricia. We don't have time to waste."

"I agree," Blaedia responded, her face grim but determined. "I'll send one of my warriors into Norithae before us, someone who can put up wards, but we need to make a move soon, before Warbotach has a chance to recuperate. Norithae was just a steppingstone for them anyway. They never intended to hold onto it."

Still leaning her weight on her lover, Aurelia listened to their conversation as though she wasn't really there, but hoping they'd start walking again soon. She was beyond antsy, the need for a shower, time with Kano, and rest, making her limbs tingle with the desperation to do something, *anything*, beside standing there. Thankfully, able to sense her emotions, Cristos wrapped up his conversation with Blaedia, pulling Aurelia closer into his side as they began walking forward again.

"What do you want to do first, love? Kano or shower? Well, after we get your arm looked at."

It was honestly a question she didn't know how to answer. She didn't have the energy for either and didn't have the mental capacity to decide.

"I'm fine. *Really.* It's not that bad. Let's just shower first so we can try to get some sleep after I visit with Kano. If I fall asleep with him, just leave me there."

Cristos chuckled and the sound of it warmed her deep within.

"There's no way I would leave you on the cold ground if you fell asleep, but you are welcome to fall asleep there."

Leaning over, he kissed her on the temple.

"I'll just have to carry you back into the tent after."

She grinned, the gesture instantly filling her with guilt.

"You know how much I love carrying you. We are going to the healer's tent first though. I don't want your arm to get infected."

After going to the healer's tent and getting her arm cleaned, stitched, and bandaged, Aurelia and Cristos showered quickly. With the aid of fae magic, the water was thankfully warm. Normally, she would have luxuriated in the warm water, would've wrapped her arms around her lover and kissed him until she was dizzy, but they were too drained, and she had to be careful not to get her fresh bandages wet. They barely shared words as they soaped their bodies and rinsed off, pulling on clean tunics and trousers. By the time they'd gotten to Kano's enclosure, the great cat wasted no time darting to the fence to greet them.

Having a clean body and clean clothes made Aurelia feel a tiny bit better, but even that filled her with guilt. She didn't even want to think about the condition her sister was in, how much Septima probably wanted a hot bath and clean clothes. The air squeezing out of her lungs, she loosened a breath as she laid the magical medallion against Kano's enclosure and entered through the opening, Cristos following behind her.

A burst of endorphins surged through Aurelia at the first touch of Kano's silky fur against her hand and the tiger nuzzled the leg of her trousers. He'd been covered in blood when she'd last seen him, so she was relieved the lanistas had bathed him, or at least given him the means to bathe himself. She checked him for wounds, passing her eyes and hands on each of his limbs, his back, and belly, but there were none. As viciously as he'd fought in the battle, as many Warbotach soldiers and horses as he'd killed, she felt foolish having been so hesitant to allow him to fight in the first place. He'd saved her life more than once that morning. He had saved many lives.

"He looks great," Cristos said as he patted the tiger on the head, Kano leaving Aurelia momentarily to lean into his touch. They both sat on the ground, Kano laying between them with his head on Aurelia's lap.

"He does. It's a relief." She hesitated, leaning her head over Kano and kissing him on the head. "I was so worried."

Scooting closer to her on the ground, Cristos wrapped his arm around her shoulder and kissed her on the cheek. Her eyes closed as she leaned into him, his warm breath skittering across her body and igniting something deep inside her.

"I know you were, love, but he's fine. We are all going to be okay. Septima will be okay, too."

Tucking further into his side, Cristos' arm around her a solid weight to ground her, she closed her eyes, his words giving her body permission to relax. She needed sleep so badly. They both did. Somewhere in that moment, with Kano's head in her lap, snoring softly, and Cristos' arm around her shoulders, her head against his chest as his intoxicating spice filled her senses, Aurelia fell asleep.

When Aurelia awoke, at what had to have been hours later, she was tucked beneath fur blankets, Cristos' warm skin smelling of sandalwood and spice flush against her back. He'd carried her there after she'd fallen asleep in Kano's enclosure just like he'd said he would.

In the windowless tent, it was impossible to see the sky outside, but Aurelia knew it was the middle of the night by the silence of the camp around them. There was nothing to do but go back to sleep, but anxiety filled her mind. How could she sleep in a warm bed when her sister was out there in the hands of their enemy? If she couldn't do anything, she could at least feel guilty.

Kicking off her blankets, she tried to get out of bed, maybe go back to Kano's enclosure and think, but warm, muscular arms wrapped around her waist and pulled her back down.

"Where are you running off to in the middle of the night?"

The gravel of his voice when fresh from sleep sent shivers into Aurelia's bones she couldn't ignore, no matter how much worry was on her shoulders. She didn't fight his affections, nuzzling into his chest as he ran his hand up her back.

"I know it's hard to do nothing, but there's nothing you *can* do right now. The best thing you can do is keep up your strength so you can fight when you need to."

Nodding against his chest, she took in his breath-taking scent. Being away from her sister was like having a missing limb but having Cristos by her side meant the world to her. They hadn't known each other for long, but it truly was as though fate had pulled them together. He was the other part of her family now, another limb she couldn't imagine losing. Her heart would truly wrench in two.

Hollowness built in Aurelia's chest, the sheer powerlessness making her limbs heavy. She knew he was right, but it was impossible to live life as usual when her sister was missing. It just felt *wrong*.

"We need to be doing something."

The backs of her eyes burned but her tears were all cried out.

"I feel like part of me is missing without her. I'm her older sister. I'm supposed to be able to protect her."

"Don't blame yourself, love. This is war. You couldn't have prevented what happened."

There were no words that could have eased her guilt, but she knew he was trying, and he meant what he said. No one blamed her for Septima's capture, but they didn't have to. At fault or not, guilt would plague her until Septima was rescued. Rolling her onto her back, Cristos leaned over her, kissing her gently.

"Blaedia has a plan, a good plan. We need her support in any move we make. She knows that kingdom better than anyone. If we barged into Aegricia now, we would die. You know it's true."

She did, but when she closed her eyes, steadying her breaths while in his arms and trying to fall back asleep, the ache in her chest remained.

Chapter 5

Aurelia

*T*he sound of voices fluttered through the darkness like spirits. Sliding her hand along the wall, she stepped forward, the need to get closer to them leading her movements. It was always night when she came here. There was never even a beam of sunlight to light her way, no light aside from the single flame she'd seen once or twice, lighting the face of who she knew to be the queen. She still didn't know how she could enter these moments in the night, nor did she know if they were anything more than a mind plagued with anxiety.

No light burned this night as she moved forward, careful not to stumble although she knew she wasn't really there. It wasn't possible. The voices grew louder as she crossed the room, but the words came less frequently the closer she got. A familiar flicker of fire came to life in the back of the room, halting her steps as the brilliant blue eyes of Otera reflected its light, and the

dark-haired figure across from the queen came into view. Before
Aurelia could reach out her hand and tell her sister they were
coming for her, the darkness returned, taking her sister with it.

Aurelia wasn't sure how long she'd stared at the darkened
ceiling of the tent, curled up in Cristos' arms as his even
breaths skittered across the top of her face, before she'd fallen
asleep as well. When she awoke, she was in the bed alone, and
the camp was busy with activity, the sounds of the other camp
residents' movements and voices making their way into the
silent tent. Her dream remained on her mind, the significance
of it not lost on her, but she had no way to know if it had
been real, and not simply her mind wishing for her sister to be
with Otera. With Blaedia having mentioned that possibility
before she'd gone to bed, it had likely been no more than her
subconscious mind seeing what it desperately wanted to see:
her sister still alive.

Although Cristos' warm skin was no longer against hers,
she realized she wasn't alone by the prickle of awareness pep-

pering her skin. Ever since they'd met, she'd always known when he was near. It didn't take long to see the electric blue eyes of her lover gazing back at her from near the water basin, a gentle smile on his handsome face bringing a smile to her own.

"Good morning."

Hanging the towel on a shelf, Cristos abandoned what he was doing and crossed the space in a few long strides, sitting beside her on the bed and leaning over to place a kiss on her lips. She closed her eyes at the touch of his mouth against hers, as though, if only in that moment, she could forget everything else.

"I hope I didn't wake you."

Aurelia shook her head and pulled him into another kiss before responding. Time stopped for a moment as his pillow-soft lips lingered.

"You didn't."

Glancing toward the entrance flap and seeing a sliver of sunshine stealing its way in, Aurelia pulled herself up on her elbows.

"Have they rung the breakfast bell yet?"

Seeming to want to keep her in bed a little longer, Cristos slid his legs beneath the blankets, forcing her to scoot over and let him lie next to her. She grinned, the temptation of a moment of pleasure too much for her to turn away with him so close, with his bare, muscular chest warming the side of her body. His skin felt like deliciously heated silk as he pulled her on top of him.

Pushing her obligations and worries aside, she submitted to him as his tongue tasted her lips and his hardness pressed against her center as she straddled him. There had always been something about him that was irresistible, like a gravitational pull from his body to hers, and she was powerless to stop it, not that she wanted to. In that moment, as he gripped her hips and pulled her against him, sliding her body along his cock and sending her nerve endings into a frenzy, she would have done anything for him.

Sliding his hands between their bodies, Cristos made quick work of the ties on Aurelia's tunic, dropping it to the floor beside their bed and wasting no time pulling her forward and sucking the peak of her breast into the hot well of his mouth. She gasped, the ecstasy of the moment such a contrast from what she'd been feeling for the past twenty-four hours. For this moment, she would allow herself to feel something other than the guilt. The feeling of his mouth on her skin, and how he trailed his tongue up the side of her neck, sent parts of her throbbing, begging for more.

"I love you," he said, the words sweet in her ear.

Expressing their love was a new thing, but it was real. She knew it was. She pulled his mouth to hers again as he fumbled with her undergarments, sliding the thin material down her thighs and tossing it over his shoulder.

They watched each other for a moment, their eyes locking as they panted. Naked on the bed, Aurelia leaned back on her elbows, and Cristos was on his knees between her legs, trousers still on but his cock straining against the inseam.

Biting her lip, she looked him over, at what pressed there.

"I want you. *Now*," she said as she reached forward and unlaced his trousers.

He watched, still breathing heavily but with an amused look on his face.

After a few moments of her struggling, he chuckled, leaning in to kiss her as he took over. He wasted no time between when he crawled over her, fitting himself between her thighs, and when he sheathed himself inside her. After the anxiety, fear, and pain of the past day, she didn't want to go slow. Not this day. She wanted him hot and hard, wanted her body so full of sensations, so full of pleasure and passion, that the hurt had no room to remain.

The tension in her belly coiled with every stroke of his hard length inside her, the slide of their bodies creating friction in all the right places. He held onto her ankles, lifting them over his shoulders as he drove into her from on his knees, his beautiful black wings spread open behind him, framing him like a god and keeping him balanced. The sight of him was all it took for Aurelia's climax to burst out of her, the ripple of pleasure making her legs stiffen against his shoulders as she screamed his name. Her body spasmed around him, squeezed the pulsing cock inside her until his body tensed and trembled, Cristos groaning with his own orgasm before falling over her, his wings tucking back in tight against his back.

There were no words, not for several moments, only the aftershocks of the intense love making—heavy breathing and soft moans, the rustling of blankets as Cristos pulled her beside him. When she slid into the crook of his shoulder, tracing her fingers along the sweat on his abdomen, her body felt boneless, like she could lay there all day. Maybe she would.

His cerulean eyes were on her when she glanced up to look at him, joyful and sated. Even after all they'd done together, she still blushed.

"I want you to be my queen, Aurelia."

Aurelia hadn't completely avoided his question, but she hadn't agreed either. The question of whether she wanted to be his queen didn't have a simple answer. She'd told him she loved him, told him they'd discuss long term plans once Septima had been found. Thankfully, the breakfast bell had interrupted the conversation she wasn't ready to have. There was no question whether she wanted to be with him. It was a resounding yes. But to rule Norithae, a kingdom she knew nothing about, to rule a kingdom at all... That gave her pause.

There was so much more to consider, including the prophecy handed down to them only weeks prior by Variel, the reclusive healer and wolf-shifter who lived in a warded cabin in Spectre Forest. The healer had known Aurelia's mother, had even been an advisor to Cristos' mother before she'd been killed, and knew more about their world than most. According to Variel, the Elemental of Spectre Forest and a powerful oracle, had prophesied: *Raging fires will fade to gentle embers, and a new day will make a new dawn. When the throne less queen falls, the phoenix will be reborn from the ashes and rise again, bringing with it unity and peace once more.*

With the prophecy being so cryptic, there were a lot of questions as to who the throne less queen was. Variel believed it was the exiled queen, Joneira, who'd murdered Aurelia's great-grandmother, the previous Aegrician queen. Aurelia's grandmother had been murdered as well. It had all been a coup to steal the Aegrician throne, but Joneira had been ousted years later and then the crown had chosen Aurelia's aunt, Otera, to rule.

Everyone had always suspected Joneira to be dead, but if the female who'd brought about Aurelia's mother's death was alive and was planning to come back and finish what she'd started... Aurelia didn't even want to think about that. The Warbotach barbarians were enough to contend with without adding in the possibility of an exiled queen and her unknown supporters.

They dressed quickly, leaving their tent and heading to the dining structure where dozens of warriors had already begun to line up. Aurelia caught Exie in the corner of her eye leaning against a tree, the warrior's eyes missing their usual zest for life. It was disheartening but not surprising. Aurelia was going through a similar stage of grief and hopelessness. Her sister and Exie had gotten very close since they'd left their father's home, first friends and then lovers. All her sister had ever wanted was to be a badass warrior and for the freedom to be with whoever she wanted to be with and not have someone else choose for her. Leaving their home had been the only way to make that happen.

With her injured leg still wrapped in bandages, Exie didn't run forward to greet them, but instead limped into the dining tent as they approached, taking her place in line behind the others.

"How did you sleep?"

Aurelia didn't expect Exie to have much of a response, at least not a positive one, but she didn't know how to initiate small talk with the situation they were in, so she chose the first question that came to her head.

Exie shrugged as she reached for her tray of porridge and roasted meat.

"I'm not sure. If it wasn't the pain in my thigh keeping me from sleep, it was the nightmares forcing me awake."

Reaching around Aurelia, Cristos took a tray for her and for himself, dipping his chin in the direction of the tables, signaling for her to lead the way. His thoughtfulness didn't go unnoticed. Her insides warmed as visions of their passion-filled morning flashed through her head, a moment of ecstasy when she was so filled with pain.

Exie aimed for their usual table near the sidewall of the dining tent where Holera and Kason were already seated, the couple eating their breakfast as they carried on a conversation. No matter how many times the camp had been moved, their table seemed to always be in roughly the same spot, and the same people always sat there. Septima's absence at breakfast was just another stab at the fresh wound.

Leaving Septima's chair empty, Exie sat across from Holera. Kason and his mate paused their conversation to look up and smile at her, but their own worried exhaustion lined their faces.

"I don't know if you've heard," Holera said, setting her spoon down in her bowl, "but we move to Norithae tomorrow to reclaim the city."

Chapter 6

Septima

Septima awoke to the squeal of an iron door hinge. The fact that she'd been taken by at least a dozen Warbotach soldiers, and not just one, had foiled her escape plan before it had even gotten off the ground. At some point, as she'd sat by that fire surrounded, someone had knocked her out.

Her head spun as she tried to sit up, her wrists and ankles no longer bound, and she blinked several times to clear her vision. She heard footsteps before she could see who was walking toward her, but when the figure passed in front of the sliver of light coming in through the window, her breath caught in her throat.

"Are you okay? I'll get you some water."

Even with her filthy, tattered dress and body that was showing signs of how long she'd been in a dungeon, Septima couldn't mistake the female for anyone other than Queen

Otera. A tear trailed down Septima's cheek as she watched Aurelia's aunt cross the darkened room and then return with a small cup of water. The queen looked so much like her sister.

Taking the cup and draining it quickly, Septima was still thirsty, and very hungry. She wasn't even sure how long it had been since she'd eaten.

"Yes. I—uh."

She quickly assessed her wrists and ankles that were scraped and bruised but nothing that wouldn't heal.

"Yes. I think so. Are you Q-Queen Otera?"

The female's eyes grew wide at the question and she searched Septima's face for a moment. Otera was beautiful. Although knotted and dirty, her hair was crimson just like Aurelia's, and hung in loose waves down her back. Even her eyes, as blue as the sea, were the eyes of her sister's. It wrenched Septima's heart open, but in another way, it soothed her.

"I am."

Otera's mouth opened to say more, but something caught her attention and she reached toward Septima, tucking her long braids behind her ear.

"You're human."

Her voice was full of wonder, disbelief, yet curiosity as well. Scooting back ever so slightly, a flicker of flame bloomed in the queen's hand as they stared at each other for several awkward moments.

"How? I don't understand."

Until that moment, Septima had not even considered that Otera wouldn't expect to see a human. Her kind hadn't been allowed in Ekromos for longer than Septima even knew, if ever. The queen may have looked human, aside from her pointed ears and the brilliant swirl of fire that danced in her palm, but she wasn't. She was fae. Septima's own sister, who she'd grown up with since she'd been taken in as an infant, was half fae, although neither of them had ever known about that part of her heritage.

"I am. My name is Septima."

"But the portal... Humans aren't allowed to cross. How did you get into our realm?"

Confusion was clear on Otera's face as she waited for her cell mate's response, which didn't come quickly.

There was so much Septima needed to tell the Aegrician queen, but she didn't know where to start, and she didn't know if they were truly alone. If there were any Warbotach spies within hearing distance, she didn't want to share any information that could put her friends and loved ones in danger. Otera must have noticed her hesitation, because she motioned for Septima to follow her toward the back wall of the space where there was another set of benches.

"As long as you speak quietly, you can speak freely here. There's a guard posted outside, but he's probably at the end of the corridor smoking his pipe or pleasuring himself. He's not exactly worried I'll escape."

Septima couldn't help but to huff a laugh, although thinking about the scar faced Warbotach beasts in any sexual manner was disgusting.

"My sister and I—."

Now it was Septima's turn to hesitate.

A dozen scenarios flitted through her mind as she debated which details to share and which to keep to herself. After a few considerations, she decided to withhold that her sister was Otera's niece, at least for the time being. If Warbotach realized Otera had family on the continent, they would surely track Aurelia down to use as leverage. It was best to keep that part a secret until she knew they wouldn't be able to use Aurelia against the queen.

"My sister and I came into this realm with your military—with Exie and Taryn, and Blaedia."

If she hadn't been able to see the queen's face with the flame still dancing in her hand, Septima may have missed how the queen's eyes lit up at the sound of Blaedia's name, at how her breath faltered.

"Blaedia? You know Blaedia?"

The reaction was unexpected, and it made Septima wonder if there was more about them she didn't know, which was likely. There was a lot she didn't know.

"Yes. I know her. Her war camp took my sister and I in when we ran away from home. She let us stay with them. She had us trained and protected. They took care of us."

Nostalgia seemed to play in the smile that spread across Otera's lips, as though she was remembering her own time with her military, or maybe someone special.

"It sounds like something they would do. They have always been an honorable representation of their kingdom."

Memory vanishing from her eyes, the queen returned her gaze to Septima.

"How did Warbotach get to you?"

Leaning back against the cold stone wall, Septima readjusted herself on one of the benches that lined the space.

"Your warriors are coming for you. We began moving toward Aegricia days ago, but a Warbotach legion caught us where Spectre Forest meets Norithae."

The clang of a rusty bolt startled Septima, effectively ending their conversation as the door creaked open. Framed by light from the sconces in the corridor, the Warbotach male in the doorway was the thing of nightmares. The scar across his face, stretching from his forehead, disappearing beneath his eyepatch, and ending at his chin, was grisly. It was almost as though he had purposely gotten it infected so it wouldn't heal well.

Septima swallowed back her grimace, along with the fear burning the back of her throat, as Otera stood in front of her. Even with the conditions she'd been living under, there was still a presence about her that told others she was a born leader and she would always rise from the ashes.

The male chuckled as he took a step into the cell, the sound guttural and almost animalistic.

"What are you gonna do, queen? Stop me from getting to the human behind you?"

Septima stiffened, her arms wrapped tightly around herself but Otera didn't back down, still blocking his view as her hands clenched into fists at her sides.

"I can certainly try."

Chapter 7

Aurelia

The army arrived at the gates of Norithae by midday. Since Blaedia had sent warriors to scout the city beforehand, they knew what to expect: a city that had been fled in a hurry. From the unburned buildings and fields, it was clear Warbotach hadn't expected the attack, at least not on the day when it happened. If they had, the city would have been left in ruins.

Instead, the citizens of Norithae crowded at the gates, lined the streets, and dropped to their knees to receive their king. His own military, weary but loyal, stood proudly, what was left of them anyway. Aurelia wasn't sure how many of Norithae's soldiers had been killed, or how many may have been taken prisoner by the barbarians, but what remained couldn't have been the entirety of what Cristos' father had built before his death.

Aurelia had never thought about the fact that Cristos' kingdom had watched him grow up, had known who he was all along, even though Warbotach hadn't. He'd hidden his identity, had walked among the barbarians as a Norithaean soldier and nothing more. She wasn't sure how he'd done it and had never asked, but the barbarians had seemed none the wiser when she'd seen him in their ranks.

Making their way through the city, she walked by his side, Kano leashed and following at her heels, with the full might of the Aegrician military behind them on foot, horseback, and as a beautiful array of phoenixes in the sky.

Exie, still injured from the gash to her leg, had begrudgingly agreed to ride on horseback. There had been some arm folding and pouting like a toddler, and not like the fierce warrior she was, but Blaedia had ultimately won the argument and the blond warrior had been hefted onto the back of a glorious black steed. Aurelia hadn't seen her since they'd left, since the animals held up the rear of the procession, but she intended to check in with her friend once they were settled in the city.

Cristos reached for Aurelia's hand as they neared the palace. It was a surreal moment. The last time she'd been there, it had been when he'd freed her and her companions from the dungeon after they'd been captured by Warbotach. She remembered their last walk through the city, when she and the others had been brought into Norithae in a cage that was pulled on a cart by a Warbotach horse.

Something about the look that had been in Cristos' eyes when she'd begged him for help told her he was good, even if she hadn't known who he was yet, or whose side he'd been on.

After only a few days, however, after Exie had been tortured, Cristos had killed the guard at the dungeon entrance and snuck them out of the city, taking them to Variel's cottage in the forest. That was where their romance had begun, and they'd been on the move ever since. Now, walking at his side toward his home, was the closing of a chapter in a way. The one thing that was missing was her sister.

"Are you okay, love?"

Squeezing Aurelia's hand gently, Cristos got her attention as they moved through the droves of people lining the streets. It wasn't a question she knew how to answer, so she simply squeezed his hand back and smiled before turning to look at the crowd again.

What truly warmed Aurelia's heart were the children, dozens of them, who stood near their parents. In their dresses and tunics, tiny leather wings flaring out at their backs, children held onto the skirts of their mothers or sat on the shoulders of their fathers. It told her the city was now safe.

Just like in Aegricia, Warbotach did not seem interested in attacking civilians, and they didn't seem interested in the kingdom of Norithae. She knew they intended to take the human lands, but she still wondered what they'd planned for the future of Ekotoria. Was Warbotach conquering Ekotoria with the help of an ally who intended to take it while they moved on to the human lands? It was a possibility that left a tinge of unease in the pit of Aurelia's stomach where everything else had gone to fester.

"They love you."

As they'd left the public spaces and entered the palace gates, it was the first thing that came to her mind. Silver lined Cristos' eyes when he turned to look at her, and she realized she'd been so caught up in her own thoughts as they'd moved through the city, that she hadn't realized how emotional it must have been for him. She stopped walking and turned to face him, pulling him into an embrace.

"They're happy to have you back, Your Highness."

Huffing a chuckle, he kissed her on the forehead.

"I just hope I don't let them down. I'm nowhere near the male my father was."

Blaedia interrupted the moment before Aurelia could respond. The military had moved in behind them in the palace courtyard, filling out nearly all the available space.

"Everyone's exhausted and needs to eat," she said, sheathing her sword. "We need to stable the horses as well."

He nodded, dipping his head to one of the Norithaean soldiers standing nearby.

The male was tall, taller even than Exie, but with silver hair like Holera's. His hazel eyes were bright in the midday sun as he approached, his hand resting on the hilt of his sword. When he stepped in front of them in full armor, his heels clicked to attention and he dipped in a bow.

"Sire."

Cristos stiffened slightly, the title clearly something he would have to get used to.

"It's still Cristos to you, Faidon."

The male dipped his head but smirked. It was clear they were friends.

"Show the Aegrician warriors to where they can house their animals and their people. We'll meet in the war room in two hours. We need to secure the city."

Faidon turned on his heel and led Blaedia and the others away, a lanista taking Kano with them. Part of Aurelia wanted to take him into the palace, but it had been a long journey and he would need to be fed. Plus, he had already become so used to living outdoors, and seemed to enjoy it. She was assured she'd be able to see him afterwards, so she patted his head and let the animal handler take him away.

Instead of following the alley which would have taken them to the dungeon, the way she'd been led the last time she had entered the city at Cristos' side, Aurelia walked into the large front doors of the palace and into the grand foyer.

Servants flitted about the space, cleaning everything within sight. They'd probably been doing just that since Warbotach had abandoned the city days before. All work ceased when Cristos walked in, every eye and smile turning in his direction.

Aurelia stepped aside as the palace staff flooded around their king, each one shaking his hand or hugging him, everyone speaking at the same time. Even with everything that had happened, she couldn't help but to giggle.

By the time they'd left the foyer of the palace, Cristos took the lead as they moved up the stairs and down a gold-paneled corridor. Aurelia could tell where artwork had been pulled from the walls, and could see the tears in the wallpaper, but the space was still beautiful.

"Warbotach inflicted a lot of damage," she said.

Cristos stopped walking to examine one of the statues that rested on a pedestal next to a set of double doors.

"They did," he responded, leaning over to kiss her on the lips, "but we'll rebuild."

It was something to look forward to—rebuilding the two kingdoms, reinstating Otera to the throne, and getting Septima back. She smiled, nodding against his chest as he pulled her close. Reaching forward, he opened one of the double doors and they stepped inside a massive bedchamber.

Unlike most of the palace, where there was evidence of the Warbotach warriors' presence, the room they entered was immaculate, fit for a royal.

"Is this your bedchamber?"

Aurelia hesitated, stepping around Cristos as he dropped their satchel and his sword on the nearest chair.

"I mean...was it your bedchamber before everything happened?"

When he turned to look at her, as he unbuttoned his cloak and dropped it with their other belongings, he was grinning. Stepping forward, he reached for her cloak, unfastening the button.

"It was."

He lifted his eyes from hers, scanning the room.

"Although it's cleaner than when I left it."

When he dropped her cloak to the chair and ran his hands up her back, she closed her eyes, leaning into him as shivers raced through her body. The day had already been long, the march from the last camp taking several hours. There was so much more to do—Aurelia knew that—but she was exhausted. Even her exhaustion was tinged in guilt, however, and sadness, for her sister who wasn't there. She had to believe

Septima was still alive, but she couldn't have known for sure. She couldn't go find her, not yet, and that left her chest in a permanent state of brokenness.

Streaming in through the window, the sun created shimmering rays of light across the center of the room, highlighting the midnight blue settee and chaise lounge that took up the center of the suite. The enormous four poster bed against one wall was large enough for her and Cristos, even considering his wings. As she scanned the room again, she realized all the furniture had been outfitted for those with wings. She guessed in a kingdom of winged people, it was to be expected.

"It is quite clean. I'm surprised it's not more damaged."

Cristos pulled away to open the balcony doors, a crisp sea breeze fluttering the curtains and filling Aurelia's nose with a mixture of brine and fresh linens.

"I suppose they didn't want to destroy the place while they were living in it. Although, the servants said only a few of the higher ranking Warbotach warriors stayed in the palace itself. The rest slept in the barracks."

Aurelia wondered how many of the Warbotach ranks stayed in Norithae, whether it had been a large proportion of their military, or if they'd simply taken the city, killed the king, and moved on. Not wanting to upset Cristos, she didn't mention it. The slain king had been his father, and Warbotach was gone, anyway.

Cristos lit the fireplace before pouring two glasses of deep red liquid from a decanter and handing one to her.

"This wine is made right here in my kingdom."

Notes of berries and a hint of apple met her nose when she lifted the glass to take a sip. It smelled remarkably like the wine she'd had in her homeland of Vaekros.

They stepped out onto the balcony, the city a flurry of activity.

"It's pleasant, reminds me a bit of home."

He watched her face for a moment, his hand settling on the small of her back, and she realized he was reading her.

"Is that a good thing?"

"There are some things about home I miss."

Turning her attention to the sea, she watched the ships sway in the harbor.

"I miss my brother more than anything, but nostalgia is a good thing. I left for Septima, though, and I don't regret that. Now, I just have to find her."

Chapter 8

Aurelia

By the time they made it down to the barracks, after grabbing a bit of bread and roasted meat from the kitchens, Blaedia and a few other Aegrician warriors were already assembled in one of the larger rooms, Taryn included. Ever since they'd been rescued from the Norithae dungeon weeks prior, the Aegrician Commander had been scarce, remaining in the background while she planned moves with Blaedia.

Aurelia smiled at her, touching her on the arm as they passed through the open doorway and around the large table in the center. She squeezed Cristos' hand before walking toward Exie who was seated on a bench on the far side of the room.

The warrior smiled as Aurelia approached, even if it had been half-hearted. Her thigh was still in bandages, the white of them a sharp contrast against the black of her fighting leathers. Aurelia lowered herself onto the bench next to Exie.

"I'd ask you if you wanted to take a walk, but—"

Not letting her finish the statement, Exie rose from the bench, reaching down a hand.

"But nothing. It's too stuffy here, anyway. Let's go."

Taking one final look at Cristos, who was standing over a large map on the table as he spoke with Blaedia, Taryn, and some of the winged Norithaean warriors, Aurelia followed Exie out the door and into the chilling evening air.

"How's the leg, Exie?"

With Exie's longer limbs, it was difficult for Aurelia to keep up with her, even with her limp. She had to walk faster to keep up.

"I hope you're taking time to rest."

Not stopping until she reached the courtyard, Exie sat down on a stone bench. Aurelia sat beside her.

"I've rested enough."

Exie couldn't seem to hide the frustration in her voice as she stretched her long legs out in front of her.

"We all have. We need to go after her."

"I understand how desperate you feel."

Reaching for Exie's hand, Aurelia squeezed it in her own.

"Finding Septima is my priority, too, but we have to be smart about it. They're meeting right now and I one hundred percent believe they'll figure out a way."

Exie blew out a breath, squeezing Aurelia's hand back.

"I know. I know they will make the best decision for the kingdom, but if I could just go after her alone…Maybe I could get her back without endangering anyone else."

Aurelia started shaking her head before Exie had even finished, but the injured warrior didn't seem to notice.

"Exie…Otera has been in the dungeon for how long? If she hasn't been able to escape yet, then you aren't going to be able to break Septima out either. I don't want to put either of them in danger in a botched escape attempt."

When Exie let go of Aurelia's hand and dropped her face into her palms, Aurelia knew she recognized her words as the truth, even if she didn't like them. Aurelia rubbed her friend's back, watching as two Norithaean soldiers walked past and toward the gates. Exie blew out a breath, smoothing her hair out of her face.

"If they don't come up with a plan soon, I'm going to go after her. I can't just sit by and do nothing."

There was nothing Exie said that Aurelia didn't feel deep within her own heart, but she was no warrior and she knew that. Where Exie may have been successful in finding a way into Aegricia and freeing her sister, Aurelia had no chance. She didn't even know how to get to the northernmost kingdom.

"I am fully on your side, Exie. We're in this together."

Smoothing her hands down her trousers, Aurelia stood before reaching down a hand.

"Come. Show me where the lanistas are keeping my tiger."

Exie rose, no argument on her tongue as she led the way around the palace and onto the grounds in the back of the enormous structure. The sun had already begun to make its descent into the horizon as they used the enchanted medallion to open Kano's enclosure. The great cat wasted no time darting forward and nuzzling Aurelia's trousers, nearly knocking her off her feet. She giggled, dropping to sit on the ground, Exie right beside her.

Aurelia and Exie stayed in Kano's enclosure until a familiar silhouette appeared from around the palace, broad shoulders framed in magnificent black wings. The grounds were dark, the sun replaced by the moon, but the torches scattered throughout set his features in firelight. Stretching, Aurelia and Exie stood. Giving Kano one more kiss on the head, Aurelia stepped out the enclosure and took Cristos by the hand, Exie following closely behind. Exie returned to the barracks, insisting on staying with the other warriors, while Cristos and Aurelia returned to his bedchambers.

There was so much on Aurelia's mind when the door clicked shut behind them. She'd missed the entire meeting between Cristos and the leaders of both kingdoms' militaries. There was undoubtedly a lot of information he would share with her, and she wanted him to, but not yet. The exhaustion of the day was weighing on her, and all she wanted to do was take a bath, and curl into her lover's arms as they fell asleep.

She hadn't even considered no longer sleeping in a tent, but it brought a smile to her face as she walked past the enormous piece of furniture and into the bathing room. Adding more wood to the fire, Cristos followed behind her, dropping his cloak on a chair as he walked by.

The sunken tub in Cristos' private bathing room was the largest she'd ever seen, even larger than what they'd bathed in when in the Diapolisian palace. Stepping around her, his hand grazing around her waist, he turned on the tap before pulling her to him. After the long day, the embrace felt amazing, his scent calming her senses.

"Was it a good meeting?" she asked, her own curiosity getting the better of her.

He grazed his nose against her cheek, nodding as he went.

"It was. The kingdom is being secured by both ground warriors and those in the sky. Blaedia is also sending scouts north toward Aegricia so they can get a better idea of how the city is being guarded."

Some of the tension in her body relaxed at his words and she leaned into him, wrapping her arms around his waist.

"So, Warbotach is truly gone from this kingdom?"

He nodded again, wrapping the laces of her tunic around his fingers as he untied them one-by-one.

"From what we can see, they are gone."

Tugging on the final tie, Cristos slid her tunic down her shoulders, dropping it to the floor.

"I have one more piece of good news."

Heart leaping in her chest, she looked into his eyes, hoping it was news about her sister but knowing deep down it wasn't.

"Yes?"

Smoothing her crimson hair off her shoulders, he slid his fingers beneath her breast band, unclasping it.

"Blaedia received word from Calista."

The pounding in her chest sped up, hope filling her while she waited for his next words.

"King Ailani is assembling his forces. There's yet to be any formal alliance, but it sounds promising."

She loosened a breath, leaning against him again.

"That's great news."

"It is something to give us hope, for sure."

Cristos pulled his tunic over his head, tossing it on top of hers.

"Would you like to bathe? I know you must be tired."

As though his words had given her body permission to rest, Aurelia yawned as she reached to unbuckle her trousers. Cristos removed his own before guiding her into the tub and stepping in behind her. Scooping up water in a copper mug, he poured it over her shoulder, the warm water relaxing her as it spread across her chest. He'd always enjoyed washing her hair, doting over her. She still didn't think she deserved a male like him, but she wasn't complaining. Methodically, Cristos wet her hair, massaging lavender shampoo into it, and she closed her eyes and savored the moment.

"Did you enjoy your time with Exie?"

The bass of his voice hit her low in her body. It always seemed to deepen at night.

Nodding, she opened her eyes to the flickering candlelight.

"She's hurting, wants to go after Septima alone."

"Hmm."

Trickles of warm water ran down Aurelia's back as Cristos rinsed her hair.

"I hope Blaedia speaks to her tonight then. It wouldn't be wise to act on impulse right now, no matter how badly she wants to."

"She knows that, and I don't think she would leave now, especially not injured."

For the remainder of their bath, Aurelia hoped she was right. If Exie did leave on her own, it could possibly put all the plans made by Cristos and the military leaders at risk. By the time they'd gotten out of the tub and climbed into bed, she'd pushed that worry to the back of her mind. It was impossible not to when her lover's scent was filling her senses.

Cristos' fingers trailed up Aurelia's stomach as they laid on the bed together, both still nude from their bath.

"One day," he said, his hand flattening on her belly.

"I hope we can have a family—you and I."

He hesitated, his fingers moving to her chin and lifting her face to look at him.

"If that's something you want, of course."

The sincerity in his eyes nearly brought her to tears. It was a beautiful thought, a future she'd never imagined. Reaching up, she took his hand in hers, kissing his palm.

"I think I would like children someday...when it's safe enough to have them."

"I'll make the world safe again, my love."

Wrapping his arms around her, he rolled her on top of him, her legs falling at his sides.

"We'll make it safer together."

When she looked into his eyes again, instead of responding, she kissed him. The touch of Cristos' body against hers consumed her as their lips pressed together, their tongues coming together in a sensual caress. His hands gripped her backside, pulling her against his hardness that was pressing in between her thighs.

"I feel like you're trying to distract me, Cristos."

Her words were merely a series of pants as she buried her face in his neck.

Pulling her against his hardness again, he chuckled.

"Is it working?"

A jolt of pleasure filled her at the friction of his skin against the most sensitive part of her and she hissed into his ear. Seeming to energize him, Cristos pulled her neck to his mouth, kissing and sucking the sensitive flesh while she ground against him. Exhaustion was replaced by urgency with every slide of him against her wetness until they were no longer able to resist, and he plunged into her.

There would be more nights where they could take their time, but after such a long and emotional day, they made love hard and fast, the sounds of their pleasure filling the entire wing of the palace. After all the time they'd spent in a camp full of tents, Aurelia didn't care.

Chapter 9

Otera

After all the time Otera had been in the dungeon below her castle, she'd never expected another person to be brought into the cell with her, and she certainly never expected to see a human face staring back at her when she first heard the guard drop someone on the other side of the room. Standing in front of the injured female, a purple knot already growing on the side of her head, Otera hoped her presence alone was enough to send the guard back out the dungeon without taking the new prisoner with him. Already injured, the human girl wouldn't stand a chance against Uldon. He'd already been losing his touch with sanity, or at least his grip on his temper.

"She needs a healer," the queen demanded, her voice resolute. "You can speak to her *after* she sees a healer."

The human female's breathing was ragged behind her, only giving the queen more of a desire to protect her. Otera knew her words didn't stand for much anymore, but she had to at least *try* to buy the girl some time. If Uldon sent in Bremusa, maybe she could get a message to her warriors. Maybe she could tell them she had Septima, let her sister know she was safe.

The guard grunted, sparing them no words before turning on his heel and leaving the cell, the heavy door slamming shut behind him. Otera pitched forward with relief, her hands bracing her on shaky knees as she sucked in breath. Reaching for Otera, Septima placed her hands on the queen's arm and guided her back onto the bench. She may have put on a brave face, but after so much time in the dungeon, Otera knew she was weaker than what she portrayed.

"Thank you."

Otera nodded, leaning against the cold stone wall as she took Septima's hand. It had been easier to live in the dungeon when she didn't have to look at the faces of her people, but having someone in the cell with her, someone to look after, that would make her life considerably more difficult. She needed to keep the young female safe, but she didn't know if she had the power to make that happen.

"You're welcome. Although I don't know how long he'll stay gone. His king isn't known for his patience."

As the guard's heavy steps retreated down the hallway, Otera loosened a breath and Septima slouched against her shoulder.

"If they send in Bremusa, we'll try to send a message to my military. I want them to know you're okay."

"Do you think that will work?"

Hope blooming in her eyes, Septima sat up a little straighter.

"Getting a message out, I mean?"

It wasn't often in Otera's long life that she'd responded to a question with a shrug, but it was all the guarantee she could give her new confidant.

"There's no guarantee. When I was first brought down here, the ravens found their way to Bremusa, which kept me more up to date on the movements of my military and my enemy's. After a while, they became fewer and fewer, until they stopped coming altogether. Whether Warbotach was shooting them down, or Blaedia stopped sending them, I'm not sure."

Something flickered in Septima's eyes, some sort of realization, something she needed to share but didn't know if she should. She remained silent a moment, before turning her deep brown eyes to Otera.

"I remember Blaedia speaking to Taryn about the ravens when my sister and I first arrived. At that time, they thought the ravens were being shot down. I overheard Blaedia saying her thoughts about it."

Hope crushing slightly in her chest, Otera slid further down on the bench and laid on her side.

"If they are being shot down, then our message may not make it through, but I'd still be willing to try—if we get the chance."

Septima nodded, laying down on the bench as well, her head nearly touching the top of Otera's. The queen cleared her throat.

"The guard may come back, or he may send a healer, but at least for now, it would be best if we tried to get some rest."

There was no response as Septima's breaths turned even, lulling Otera's own exhausted mind to sleep as well.

Chapter 10

Aurelia

"I want them to know you're okay."

Queen Otera leaned against the stone wall of the dungeon, her fingers interlaced with the woman at her side. Aurelia watched from the shadows of her mind, which were also the shadows of the room. She was still unsure whether what she was experiencing was real or a dream. If what she saw in her mind was real, Septima was safe, but there was no guarantee she would remain that way. Although Aurelia didn't know what Warbotach knew, they had an interest in speaking to her sister, and it was only a matter of time before the guard who'd only just left would return. All she could do was hope Otera could keep Septima safe until they could free them both.

Aurelia watched them for a while. She listened as Septima told the queen what she knew about the ravens, and as they laid on the bench beside each other like the oldest of friends.

She remained there until her sister fell asleep, cherishing every moment she got to glimpse her sister's beautiful face, even if it was only a dream.

When Aurelia awoke the next morning, it took her a moment to realize where she was. With silk sheets against her bare flesh and the scent of fresh linens, the only thing familiar was the warm body of Cristos next to her. It almost felt wrong, waking up in such comfort when she knew her sister was in a dungeon, but there was nothing she could do to change Septima's circumstances. At least not yet. She had to trust in the process, trust that Cristos and the generals were in control of the situation, and that their plans would get her sister back safely. It was the only way she could continue her day without Septima by her side.

The fire had nearly burned down to the grate when Cristos' eyes opened. Aurelia had been watching him sleep for a while, unable to resist when he looked so peaceful. With all their recent travel, his ebony hair had grown long, nearly falling into his eyes as his brilliant blue gaze met her own.

"Good morning."

His voice was still rough from sleep and the ruggedness of it sent a shiver through her, as it always did.

"Good morning."

Tucking her hair behind her ear, he leaned forward and kissed her.

"What's the plan for today? More meetings?"

As if on cue, a knock sounded on the suite's door. Cristos' eyes flicked up, mild annoyance on his face as he rose from the bed, pulling on a pair of trousers and answering the door. Still undressed, Aurelia wrapped the sheet around her body and ran behind the dressing screen, pulling on a tunic and trousers quickly before returning to Cristos' side. If they were discussing going into Aegricia, she wanted to be there when they did.

The same soldier she'd seen only briefly when they'd arrived, Faidon, stood there in full uniform, his hand on the pommel of his sword.

"The Aegrician flyers have returned, Cristos. General Ryze requests a meeting."

Having never heard Blaedia's full name, it took Aurelia a moment to realize who he was speaking of. Come to think of it, she didn't know any of her newfound family's surnames, aside from the true surname of her mother, the anticipated queen of Aegricia before she'd been chased out of her kingdom and murdered: *Lumino*. Aurelia swallowed back the thought as Cristos turned to her, the warrior pivoting on his heel and walking away.

His boyish early morning appearance replaced by that of a king, Cristos braced his hands on her shoulders.

"I guess my trial as a ruler truly begins today. Ready or not."

Even if he doubted his capability as a king, Aurelia didn't. The passion he held for his kingdom would have never allowed him to act in any way that wasn't in its best interest. She smiled, rising to his toes and kissing him.

"You are ready, and you won't be ruling alone. Like it or not, you have two kingdoms at your side...and you have me."

It wasn't a promise to be his queen, but they both understood that. Married or not, they were in this fight together. The rest would have to come later. He took her hand, squeezing it gently.

"And that's how we will win this war—all of us—together."

Taking only enough time to eat eggs and toast, Aurelia and Cristos left the palace for the barracks, arriving just as Blaedia and the Norithaean generals gathered around the map on the table in the center of the room. Having not taken part in the meeting the night before, Aurelia didn't know the names of the leaders from Cristos' kingdom, but she knew she'd get to know them in time.

Instead of standing around the table, where the bodies with wings already took up so much space, she moved to the other side of the room where the familiar head of blond hair leaned against the wall. Holera sat beside Exie, the two of them deep in conversation as Kason held his own conversation with one of the Norithaean warriors. Taking a seat next to the two females, Aurelia listened as the Aegricians and Norithaeans readied to discuss their next course of action.

"The city of Flamecliff is completely surrounded, but the city itself is warded," Blaedia said, Cristos' expression visibly tense. "My warriors were turned around at the gates. The wards go into the clouds and beyond."

Heart sinking into her stomach, Aurelia reached for Exie's hand. Septima was unreachable without war. She knew it, and Exie knew it too.

Cristos paced as Blaedia and Taryn looked over the map, a dark haired Norithaean officer doing the same.

"Is there any way to take the wards down?"

The Aegrician general listened as one of her warriors spoke something into her ear before turning back to Cristos.

"There may be a way to take them down if there are enough of us, but we may have bigger problems to contend with."

Blood chilled in Aurelia's veins as Exie tightened the grip on her hand. Cristos stiffened as he turned to the general, her words putting an end to his pacing.

"What could be a bigger problem than Warbotach?"

Her face resembling something Aurelia had only ever seen on the general before their last battle, it was clear Blaedia didn't want to say out loud whatever she'd been told.

"There have been sightings across the sea, mutterings of armies from the other continents encroaching on Ekotoria."

Swearing, Cristos combed his hands through his hair. Aurelia's breath faltered. She didn't know anything about the other continents in the fae realm, aside from what Exie and Cristos had discussed briefly one night when they'd sat in Kano's enclosure. There were other continents with other rulers, but even Cristos had admitted to knowing little about them.

"We'll send out flyers today, and ravens. We need to know what we're up against, and how much time we have."

He turned toward Faidon, the weight of his decisions lining his handsome face.

"We'll need to notify King Ailani. We cannot wait any longer for his decision, not if we're going to prevent this continent from falling from the armies that may be heading toward our shores. I think we will know soon who Uldon is receiving support from, or who he's running from."

Before Cristos finished speaking, Exie stood and stormed out of the room without a word. Holera, who had been silent during the meeting, followed behind her. Aurelia hesitated, but only a moment, before following her friend. She wanted to remain in the meeting and continue listening to what Cristos and the leaders of the two kingdoms would plan, but Exie needed her more. Aside from herself, she knew Exie had her sister's best interest at heart above all others.

Once outside, it didn't take Aurelia long to find her friend. Sitting on the same bench in the courtyard where they'd spoken the day before, Exie's golden hair glowed in the sunlight as she spoke with Holera. Aurelia didn't have to talk to Exie to know why silver lined her friend's honey-colored eyes. Enemies flooding onto Ekotoria's shores would only make rescuing Septima that much more impossible, even without the wards. It had remained unsaid in Blaedia and Cristos' discussions, along with freeing the queen, but everyone knew turning their sights to the shores and away from Aegricia was a tradeoff they would have to make, at least until they knew more about the possible threat the rumors posed.

Blowing out a breath, Aurelia took the last few steps toward her friends and lowered herself onto the bench next to them. Exie glanced up at her, the corner of her mouth lifting in a forced smile.

"She's still safe, Exie. I saw it."

She'd never mentioned her dreams to Exie before, but her friend needed hope.

Exie searched her face for a moment before responding.

"What do you mean you saw it? How?"

It was a question Aurelia didn't know how to answer but she couldn't just leave it in the air.

"I don't know how it happens, or if it's even real, but the more I see Otera in my dreams, the more I wonder if I'm seeing her, the real her. If it is real, then Septima is with her, and she's protecting her."

Holera leaned forward, resting her elbows on her knees. Exie exhaled before speaking.

"What have you seen, Aurelia? Specifically."

Taking Exie by the hand, Aurelia told her friends everything she could recall. She began with the very first vision she had of her aunt when she'd first entered their camp after fleeing her father's home. The more she spoke, the larger their eyes grew.

"Variel spoke of this happening, when she told us about your mother."

It had seemed like a lifetime ago, and Aurelia tried to replay the conversation Exie spoke of in her head, but to no avail.

That entire day had been too much for her to comprehend, and their lives hadn't slowed down since then so she could have time to reflect. She shook her head, and Exie took that as permission to continue.

"She and Cristos said you may come into powers over time. Maybe that's what this is, powers from your mother's blood revealing themselves as you begin to transition."

Aurelia swallowed around the growing lump in her throat as Cristos and Variel's words found their way into her memory. There was no question of the truth about her mother, not after seeing her mother's reflection in Otera's face, but to acknowledge her own body was anything other than human...It wasn't something Aurelia had ever considered, no matter how true she knew it to be.

"So, do you think what I'm seeing is real?"

Although she already knew the answer, she still asked. When she lifted her eyes to her friends, her answer was confirmed.

"How will I know when my transformation is complete?"

Exie shrugged, but Holera answered.

"With no other humans in our realm, there's no way to know what level of powers you'll develop, or if you'll see any physical changes."

"There's one person who may be able to answer your questions, though," Exie added, Aurelia turning a curious glance to her.

"Who?"

"Variel."

Chapter 11

Aurelia

Exie's words weighed heavily on Aurelia as she and Cristos returned to their suite that night. Twelve warriors had been sent out that afternoon, some from each kingdom. Ten of the warriors had been given orders to search the seas to try to find out more about the alleged armies heading to Ekotoria. Kason and Holera had been sent straight to Diapolis to demand an audience with King Ailani, and to hopefully return with his army, and his dragons, at their backs. After their recent trip to the southern kingdom, Cristos realized the couple were the best people to send to seek that meeting.

The idea of returning to Variel's cottage in the woods with everything that was happening, if she could even find it, was unthinkable. She wouldn't have been able to pull Cristos away from his kingdom in the middle of a war, but if learning about her powers could somehow aid them in winning the war... There was no guarantee that would be the case, but if it was at all possible, she knew she needed to explore it. Still, she wasn't ready to leave just yet, not after merely a day, and not after having been captured from Spectre Forest only weeks earlier. She'd been thrown into the dungeon in the very palace where she now slept. If Warbotach had warriors hiding in the forest, she did not want to become their prisoner again. Her sister needed to be her number one priority, and being thrown into a dungeon, even if it was the same dungeon as Septima, would only make rescue more impossible.

After talking with Exie and Holera, Aurelia had gone to Kano's enclosure, putting the large tiger on a leash and taking him for a walk around the palace grounds. With everything she and her friends had talked about, she really needed to clear her head. Although Kano received more than just a few passing glances from the staff and soldiers, he seemed to enjoy his time out of the confines of his enclosure. He tested the limits of his leash more than once, chasing after small creatures as they traversed the forested area at the back of the property and climbing over boulders scattered along the cliff that overlooked the sea.

She'd returned him to his enclosure just before dark and returned to the palace and Cristos' side.

Sitting next to her on the settee, Cristos passed Aurelia a glass of wine, the red liquid tart on her tongue. She was tired. They both were, but the palace staff had been asked to bring their dinner up to their room that night, so they couldn't go to sleep just yet.

A fire flickered in the grate, warming her chilled limbs from spending so much time in the cool Norithaean breeze. They were quiet for a while, Aurelia's feet in Cristos' lap as they waited for their dinner to be brought up.

"What happened with Exie today...when she ran out?"

Cristos' voice broke the silence, and Aurelia's endless thoughts.

"I know these new developments can't be easy for either of you, not with Septima being stuck behind those wards."

Aurelia shrugged before responding, her mind needing a moment to gather her thoughts.

"I think she just feels hopeless. We both do. With the wards, she knows she can't go after Septima. It took away that option."

Nodding, he rubbed her feet.

"We will get her back, Aurelia. This I promise you. With this new threat, King Ailani will help us. I have to believe that."

Even if she wasn't confident in the future of the continent, she knew he truly believed what he said.

"She's just never seemed further away, more unattainable."

A knock sounded on the door before he responded and Cristos rose to answer. He returned a moment later with a platter holding their dinner and placed it on the table. At least for the moment, Aurelia dropped the conversation. There was nothing they could do to get Septima back yet. She was hungry and she was tired, so that conversation would have to wait until another time, along with the conversation about revisiting Variel.

"How do you feel about stew?" he asked as he opened the lid on the pot, the savory scent of the meat and vegetable stew wafting through the air. It reminded her of the meals they'd eaten back at the Aegrician war camp for all the time they'd lived there.

Cristos pulled out Aurelia's chair and she lowered into it before he slid her closer to the table. Her mouth watered and she realized it had been hours since she'd had anything to eat.

"Stew sounds great. I don't think we've had any since we were in the forest camp. Actually—"

Hesitating, she took in a deep whiff of the scent.

"It smells a lot like Aegrician stew."

He chuckled as he lowered himself into his chair and filled two bowls, sliding one in front of her.

"That's because it *is* Aegrician stew. The cooks from the camp cooked for us tonight and brought it in. They thought you would like that, and I agreed."

The grin on his face told her he knew he'd done something good. The camp had begun to feel like home, but the palace was not home yet, so he'd brought something from home to her. Cristos was such a thoughtful male, one who always found a way to take care of her, even when she couldn't think about herself.

She smiled back at him, taking a bite of the steaming meal, the bits of meat and vegetables tender and flavorful.

"Thank you for thinking of this. It makes me miss my sister a little more, but that camp was home to us for a while. It was where we felt safe."

The corner of his mouth tugging up, Cristos reached across the table and took her hand, kissing her on the knuckles.

"It was the first place we'd ever been together, *made love*. The Aegrician camp was the first place I realized I loved you, realized you were meant to be my bonded mate."

Aurelia froze, the words *bonded mate* hitting her by surprise. They were lovers, yes, and even hoped to get married one day, but mates, as seen by the fae, were something so much more. She stumbled over her words for a moment, the right response failing her.

"Mate? Bonded mate?"

The change in his expression sent a dull pain in her heart. He looked almost...rejected.

"I know it's not a human tradition, and it's not something that humans feel, but it is something that happens for the fae."

Lifting her hand to his face, he rubbed it along his cheek, his eyes falling closed as her skin caressed through his stubble.

"When the fates decide that two people are bonded mates, their bodies tell them it is true. It's a draw to that person that you can't deny. As a half-human, maybe you hadn't felt it, maybe you won't unless you transition into more of your fae blood, but I have felt it."

His words confused her. If he'd felt they were mates, why hadn't he told her? Maybe he had and she hadn't understood. There was still so much about their world she didn't know. She squeezed her eyes shut, her mind trying to remember his words, trying to see the signs she may have not noticed.

"When did you feel this?"

Smiling, he kissed her knuckles again, but she could see the sadness in his eyes, the rejection he felt that she didn't want him to feel at all. It broke her heart that she'd made him feel that way, even if she hadn't intended to.

"In Variel's cabin when I was fixing your bathwater and you touched me."

He hesitated, his blue eyes darkening.

"When you passed by me, your shoulder brushed against my wing, and I felt the surge of the bond. When I laid down on the bedroll to sleep, I knew you were my bonded mate, even if you didn't, and it was all I could think about."

She shook her head, not to deny him but to make her head remember. Although he hadn't said anything to her, she'd noticed how he stiffened when she'd brushed into his wing right before he'd laid down on the bedroll and appeared to go to sleep. Even then, she'd known something had changed between them after that moment. She'd noticed a temporary change in his demeanor.

"Why didn't you tell me?"

"There were many reasons why I didn't tell you. We'd only just met, and you were human. I knew humans didn't have bonded mates, so I didn't think you would understand, and I didn't want to scare you off. Also, since you were human, I knew you probably wouldn't have felt the bond, so I may have been bonded to you, but I didn't know if you'd ever acknowledge being bonded to me."

Standing from the table, he moved his chair closer until their knees were touching, taking both her hands in his.

"After that night, Variel told you about your mom and I didn't want to add to the overwhelming amount of information that had already been dumped on you. Once we left Variel's, we'd gotten attacked, had gone to Diapolis, and then everything that had happened there, then the attack on the way back from Diapolis before immediately going into war... It had never been a good time. Not until now."

The entire time he'd known they were fated for each other but hadn't told her. It was another truth he'd kept from her, but she understood why he did it. She had been overwhelmed at Variel's cottage, and they had gone through so much in so little time. It would have been too much to process, but had she known they were mates, she would have never had to wonder what their future would be. She thought about all the times she'd told herself she would never work as his queen because she was human, but it had never even been an option to say no, not if they were bonded mates. If they were bonded mates, then they belonged to each other and they would be together forever. It wasn't such a bad thought.

Cristos watched her, his eyes expectant. He loved her so much. There was no question.

"I understand why you didn't tell me," she said, leaning forward to kiss him, her lips lingering for a moment longer. "But now that I know, I suppose you expect me to marry you and be your queen."

Smirking, he pulled her onto his lap.

ing without trying to take her with him. After the standoff between the guard and Otera the night before, she had been dreading the Warbotach guard's return.

"I'm here to look over her wounds," Bremusa said, motioning to Septima. "I have fresh clothes for both of you, and water for a bath."

Otera huffed as she leaned forward to take what Bremusa was carrying and set it on the bench beside her.

"What's the occasion for fresh clothes and a bath? That's not Uldon's style."

"He doesn't tell me his reasons, Your Majesty. They just give me the orders."

Moving toward Septima, Bremusa lowered herself onto the bench beside her.

"Can I check your head?"

Nodding, Septima slid her braids to the side to show Bremusa the spot on her head that was still sore from where she'd been hit.

"It's not as bad as it was," she said through clenched teeth as the healer touched a tender spot. "My head is clearer this morning. I'm not as dizzy."

Otera stood, reaching into the barrel and dampening a rag before handing it to Bremusa. The elderly female took it and proceeded to clean Septima's scalp gently, taking her time as she wiped around the root of each braid. Behind her, the queen had unbuttoned her dress and begun wiping herself down with another rag. Septima tried to not look at how Otera's ribs protruded so blatantly, but it was hard to look away. The queen needed to get out of the dungeon. They both did.

"What's your name?"

So lost in her thoughts, Septima hadn't even noticed that Bremusa had stopped cleaning her hair.

She cleared her throat, eyes shifting away from the queen who had pulled on one of the simple white dresses they'd been given.

"Septima. My name is Septima."

Bremusa leaned forward, the cloth moving to wipe the dirt from her face.

"And you came from the human realm, Septima?"

The question churned in her gut, but she nodded.

"And you have family on this continent, or did you come alone?"

Telling anyone else about Aurelia would put her at risk, so Septima hesitated. Otera noticed the turn of the conversation and sat next to her, the queen finished dressing and finger combing her long crimson locks.

"Let's get Septima cleaned up and changed before the beasts return for you and the water," she said, reaching for Septima's hand. "We can talk more when we are no longer at risk of being overheard."

The guard returned a short time later, removing the barrel and Bremusa, but leaving Septima and Otera where they were. Septima exhaled a breath of relief as the heavy door squealed shut and the bolt on the outside clanged into place. She didn't know why the guard hadn't demanded to take her with him as he had done the night before, but she wasn't going to get her hopes up that he wouldn't return for her that night, or even the next day. All she could do was hope.

A meager breakfast had been left for them, plates with bread and cheese, along with glasses of water, had been laid on the bench near the window. They sat beside each other, nibbling on the little food they had as the sliver of sunlight warmed the chilly cellar.

"Bremusa is a very old friend of mine," Otera said, her voice just over a whisper in case the guard was listening outside the door. "My sister..." She hesitated, the queen's eyes going distance for a moment. "My sister, Messalina, and I have known Bremusa since we were children."

Hearing her mother's name, Aurelia's mother's name, threatened to rip Septima's heart in two. Messalina hadn't been Septima's mother by birth, and she'd died before Septima was only a toddler, but she still loved her, and mourned the life she could have had with her. She knew Aurelia missed her mother every day. For a moment, Septima thought about telling Otera that Messalina was her mother, but she couldn't, not yet, not if it would put Aurelia at risk.

"How long have you been here? In the dungeon, I mean."

The queen hesitated for a minute, glancing toward something at the back of the stone room that Septima couldn't see.

"A few months, although 1 admittedly lost count. Time seems to stand still in this room."

"Do you ever get to leave?"

Septima couldn't imagine being stuck in that dungeon for months. Just the thought of that happening, of them not being rescued soon, caused her stomach to churn.

"Uldon has summoned me on a few occasions, mostly so he can brag, or rave like a lunatic. He's becoming quite un-hinged, so we really are safer here until we get free."

It made sense. If the Warbotach king really was losing control of his sanity, or simply his temper, then stone walls separating him from them was a deterrent, even if it would only give them a false sense of security. Uldon had a key to their cell, after all. All he'd have to do is use the key and then they would no longer be safer from him than if they'd been standing in his chambers.

"So, what is our plan? I know you were unable to talk to Bremusa about contacting Blaedia and the rest of the military, since we were worried about being overheard-"

"Bremusa," Otera cut her off. "Knows things most people don't. I didn't need to tell her for her to already know exactly what I needed her to do. If she can find a way to send that message, she will. I have total confidence in her."

Otera's words settled Septima's stomach, if only a little.

"How well do you know Blaedia and Taryn—oh, and Exie?"

A smile lifting on the queen's lips, Otera pulled her legs onto the bench beneath her and crossed them as though she were sitting on the grass outside. Septima leaned against the wall, pulling her knees to her chest.

"I know all three of them *very* well. Blaedia is my mate, and I miss her terribly, more than anyone."

The admission took Septima by surprise, but she didn't interrupt.

"Taryn has been in my military for as long as Blaedia has, for as long as I've been queen. Exie came from a class behind them. She and Holera trained in the same group, but under Blaedia as my general."

Hearing the queen speak so openly about her love life encouraged Septima to share with her as well, if only about that. She still wasn't ready to disclose her sister's identity yet.

"Exie and I are together," she admitted, feeling her cheeks heat as soon as the words left her mouth. "I love her very much and I hate how much she must be worrying."

Taking Septima by the hand, Otera's blue eyes softened even more.

"Exie is a good female—a bit wild and unruly some-times—but as loyal as they come. I promise Exie is probably trying her best to find a way to rescue you. After everything she's been through, she wouldn't be one who'd be able to just sit by and wait."

Septima didn't want to outright ask what Otera was referring to, but the queen seemed to notice her confusion.

"Her lover, a female she thought was her mate, died many years ago. It hit Exie very hard and I worried she'd never be the same again, but she's resilient, and has grown through her grief."

The tear in Septima's heart throbbed at learning the woman she loved had not only loved before but had lost in such a horrible way. Losing someone by choice would have been so much easier than losing someone because of death. Exie had never disclosed anything about her lover dying, but Septima realized it was probably because it had been too painful to bring it up. When Exie was ready to talk about her loss, Septima knew she would be there for her.

Chapter 13

Kason

Kason and Holera, along with eight other warriors from the combined kingdoms, had left Norithae only hours after the meeting where they'd learned about the added potential threat to their borders. Since they'd recently returned from an envoy to the seaside kingdom, Blaedia and Cristos had agreed that sending the mated pair back to speak to King Ailani was the best choice. After decades together, Kason and Holera did nearly everything together, and Kason had a way about him that tended to get things done. If anyone could give the hesitant king the nudge he needed, Kason was that person.

Aside from meeting with King Ailani, their other task was to bring their missing healer, Calista, back to Norithae. Calista had been sent to notify King Ailani of the Warbotach attack on his border town weeks prior, when they had been

involved in the attack on their returning trip from his kingdom, and she'd yet to return to the Aegrician camp. They
had received a communication from Calista, but Blaedia was
concerned she was being held by the king for some sort of
insurance, and if that was the case, she needed to be retrieved.

There was no way to know if that was the case until they
spoke to Calista, but if King Ailani was holding one of their
healers against her will, Aegricia would have bigger problems
to deal with than just Warbotach and the enemy ships closing
in on them from other continents.

The trip from Norithae to Diapolis was extensive, especially since they were unable to fly all the way into the capital
city of Embershell. Although Holera could physically fly the
whole route, with breaks in between, King Ailani held the
last of the continent's dragons, and the beasts patrolled his
kingdom extensively. Even with sending prior notice to the
king about their impending arrival, there was no way to know
if the dragons would see the approaching phoenix as a friend
instead of an enemy, so they were always instructed to handle
the final leg of the journey on horseback. It made the trip
longer, but it was safer.

Riding on the back of his mate in her phoenix form, as Kason had done for the past nearly three decades, he stroked Holera's silver feathers as her mighty wings worked against the chilled wind over the Elder Sea. As they'd done on their last trip to Diapolis, they hoped to make it to the southern-most part of Spectre Forest before stopping to camp for the night. Leaving from Norithae, which was on the northern part of the continent, was a farther journey on the first day than what they'd achieved last time, but they'd certainly faced larger feats than that, so he and his mate were hopeful they could handle the extensive hours in the air.

Kason watched the water as they traveled, admiring the beauty of his continent while hoping it wouldn't be destroyed in the coming days or weeks. Ever since the exiled queen, Joneira, had stolen the Aegrician throne more than twenty years ago, there had been few years of relative peace on their continent.

Otera's rule had been prosperous, once Joneira had been ousted, but there had always been the threat of Warbotach from the dead region of Ekotoria, and there had always been the fear that Joneira would return. Kason had never believed any of the speculation that she was dead. She was simply biding her time until she could return and take it all.

Huffing out a breath and shifting his weight, he watched the edge of Spectre Forest come into view as the sun began to set over the edges of his world. The further south they flew, the warmer the air became.

Holera's wings leveled out as they turned back toward the land, sailing across the breeze along the coast, the wind nearly pulling Kason's long hair from the band holding it at his nape. He rubbed at Holera's silver feathers on her neck again, wishing it was the warmth of her ivory skin against his palm instead. Just thinking about it made his cock begin to stiffen in his leathers. He truly was the luckiest of males to have her in his life.

"We're almost there, my fierce beauty."

She couldn't speak to him in her phoenix form, but her chest rumbled below his hand telling him she'd heard him. Grinning to himself, he continued to stroke her neck, the need to touch her one he'd never gotten over, and never would.

"I look forward to staying at the inn tomorrow. You deserve a soft bed for the night."

He meant every word and she knew it. The thick tree canopy of Spectre Forest thinned as they reached the edges of the forest, giving Holera the perfect opportunity to land. They touched down in a clearing with the grace of a songbird, Kason jumping down from his mate so she could stretch her massive body and shift into one with much more seductive curves.

Dropping their bags on the dirt at his feet, he approached her as she shifted, sliding his strong hands up her back.

"You must be tired. I'll set up camp."

Holera grinned, pulling him by the front of his shirt to kiss him. He groaned against her lips.

"You relax."

"You know I've never been a fair maiden needing coddling," she said as she reached for branches, tossing them into a pile for a fire. "You can set up the tent, but I can collect firewood. I'm tired, but I'll rest after."

Watching for a moment, Kason smirked at her as she reached for another fallen branch and stuck out her tongue at him. She truly was the most stubborn of females. He'd been trying to take care of her from the start, but she always insisted on taking care of herself. One day, he told himself as he pulled their tent from a bag and placed it on the ground. One day, when their continent was at peace, he would fill her with his child and she would let him place her on the pedestal she deserved, if only for a little while.

Although Holera had claimed to have more energy to spare after their long flight from Norithae to the edges of Spectre Forest, she had fallen asleep against Kason's chest as they'd sat before the fire eating some of the dried meat and bread they'd brought. Carrying her into the tent and covering her had filled him with pride, and he'd watched her slumber for a while, caressing her hair as her chest rose and fell with the gentle breaths of sleep.

When they woke the next morning, after taking a moment to eat and pack their belongings, they set off for the second part of their journey by air. Although they'd taken the entire kingdom of Diapolis on foot when they'd journeyed south with Cristos, Calista, and Aurelia, Kason and Holera opted to travel to the border town of Claywind by air since they were traveling alone. Once there, they would have to buy horses for the rest of their trip. In Claywind, they planned to rent a room at the inn for the night, something Kason was looking forward to. With as uncertain as Ekotoria's future was, a warm bed to make love to his mate, good food, and strong whiskey, would be a welcomed release.

Although the town of Claywind was part of the Diapolisian kingdom, it couldn't have been more different from the capital city on the coast. Made up of merely a strip of structures at the town's center, and farms or ranches along the lone road that passed through, they would have flown over it without noticing had they not known it was there. The one thing that had changed since their last visit was that many of the buildings had been left as nothing more than charred remains after the attack by Warbotach weeks earlier.

By the time they landed on the road in front of the tavern, which had not been destroyed, the sun was already beginning to set, painting the sky in a beautiful array of pastels. Kason tossed his and Holera's weapons, as well as their packs, over his shoulder, leaving his lover to walk unencumbered. She never complained, but he knew carrying his weight couldn't have been easy, even if she was massive as a phoenix.

Grinning at her as she walked next to him, he gave her a single wink before scooping her up in his arms. She swatted at him, but only haphazardly, before giving up and going limp against his chest.

"I told you I didn't need coddling, you big brute."

Kason chuckled as he kissed her on the forehead.

"Just because you don't need coddling, my beautiful warrior, doesn't mean you won't get it."

Leaning forward, Holera grasped the handle of the tavern door and pulled it open as Kason carried her inside. The smell of roasting meat and the sound of live music greeted them as they entered, and Kason set his lover down near a small table in the corner before pulling out her chair.

"I'll go speak to the bartender about a room," he said, dropping the packs on the floor by the table. "I'll be right back."

Holera didn't argue as Kason walked away, sitting in one of the chairs and propping her feet up on the other. Even if she didn't complain, Kason knew she was tired. Over the past few weeks, they'd done nothing but train, fight, and travel. She may have been a warrior, but it was a lot for anyone to handle in such a short period of time.

Chapter 14

Kason

After filling up on roasted meat and vegetables, and enjoying a stout glass of whiskey, Kason and Holera ascended the stairs to the second level and retired to their room for the night. Knowing they would be requesting an audience with the Diapolisian king the next day placed a heavy weight on Kason's shoulders, a weight the whiskey had been unable to ease. He tried not to let his own stress show as he ran Holera's bath, but he worried they would not leave Diapolis with the king's support, or that they would not leave Diapolis at all.

"You're distracted."

Watching the warm water fill the tub and lost in his own thoughts, Holera's voice caught Kason by surprise. When he turned to look at her, her brilliant violet eyes searched his face.

She pulled the first lace of her leathers loose, the top sliding open to reveal her perfect ivory skin.

Abandoning everything he'd been dwelling on, he rose and pulled her to him.

"I *was* distracted. I'm not anymore."

His mate was always so reserved around others, but the mischievous grin she saved for only him pulled a rumble from his chest. Leaning forward, he kissed the skin peeking through the opening in her leathers before untying the rest of the laces until her top slid down her shoulders.

Gentle fingers cupping his chin, she forced him to look at her.

"What's on your mind?"

He chuckled, nuzzling into her neck.

"At the moment, all I'm thinking about is your skin on my tongue."

Although he knew his refusal to tell her what was really on his mind frustrated her, it only took a few moments of his kisses against her neck and she'd abandoned all demands of talking. After three decades together, he knew exactly what he needed to do to distract her as well, so he lifted her, carrying her into the bedchamber and placing her on the bed.

Crawling over his mate's body like a hungry predator was one of Kason's favorite things to do, and he didn't care if she'd bathed yet or not. She would get her bath, but he couldn't wait any longer to touch her.

Holera groaned, rubbing her fingers up his back as he kissed her neck.

"I thought I was going to take a bath."

The way her warm breath fanned across his ear nearly made him come undone. Sliding his hand around her ankle, he wrapped her leg around his hip before grinding his hardened length against her center. She hissed, digging her nails into his backside and pulling him closer.

"You can bathe after. I like you a little dirty."

A breathy hum came out of Holera as she leaned up and took Kason's bottom lip into her mouth, sucking gently until he opened for her and kissed her deeply, hungrily. His hands caressed the curves of her breasts, tracing down her flat stomach before gripping her hips and holding her in place as he dragged his cock against her again.

Wrapping her other long leg around his waist, she flipped them over, straddling him as he laid on his back, her hands going to the buckle of his pants.

"If you want me dirty," she said, her voice husky and full of need as she undid the buckle on his pants, the clasp falling open to reveal the dark hair below his belly button, "Then I want you naked."

He chuckled, wasting no time to flip her back over and slide his pants down his hips, kicking them to the floor before helping his mate remove the remainder of her clothes. Never hesitant to demand what she wanted from him, Holera reached between them, fitting his hardness at her entrance before wrapping her legs around his hips, pulling him into her warmth.

Kason groaned, sliding his fingers into his mate's silver hair and pulling her lips to his, his tongue caressing hers in a sensual dance, only building their need for each other. They moved together, Holera's body squeezing his cock exquisitely, driving him nearly over the edge but he clenched his teeth, giving his body no choice but to delay his climax until his mate had gotten hers. No matter how little time they had, he always insisted she get her pleasure first. It meant way more to him than his own needs.

Draping her beautifully long legs over his shoulder, Kason rose onto his knees, gripping her hips and lifting them so he could drive his cock into her at just the right angle to make her orgasm shatter through her at a level that would have her still feeling the effects the next day. He wanted her to scream his name so loud the patrons would hear it downstairs in the tavern.

Holera's natural scent, mixed with the sweet scent of her arousal, had him drunk and he growled, leaning back over her and taking her hands in his own. She didn't argue as Kason guided her arms over her head and had her grip the headboard.

"Hold on, my fierce mate."

Her violet eyes flared with lust as she did as he asked, gripping the headboard with both hands while Kason lifted her legs and drove into her, *hard*. Holera screamed his name, her orgasm hitting her quickly, her cunt squeezing him inside her and sending him over the edge. When they were spent, Kason collapsed over his mate's body, sweat drenching them both.

Chapter 15

Taryn

hapter 15

Taryn

C Flapping her great crimson wings, Taryn led a group of ten warriors over the Spectre Forest toward the western side of the continent. They'd been flying for hours but didn't intend to stop and sleep until nightfall. Five Norithae warriors flanked her own warriors in the sky, three males and two females, all flying toward the setting sun. Letting out a keening sound, the only way she could communicate in her phoenix form, she leveled out her wings, allowing herself to coast down toward an opening in the tree canopy. The rest of the group followed her lead.

Setting down as the light faded from the sky, a few of the warriors gathered firewood while others put up the tents. Taryn and Silia, one of her lieutenants, walked the perimeter, putting up cloaking wards around the space they would call home for the night. With time being of the essence, they couldn't stop for long, but they needed to at least get a few hours of rest before continuing to the coast.

"What do you think we'll find once we get across the continent?"

The last of the wards erected around the camp, strong enough to last until daylight, Silia turned to Taryn, her eyes heavy with exhaustion.

It was the same question Taryn had been asking herself since they'd gotten the news about the armada heading to their shores, but she feared the answer, not for herself but for her people. If Ekotoria was invaded again, she didn't think they would be able to survive it, even if Diapolis sent in troops to help them. Their chances were far worse than she wanted to admit.

"Aside from the Inferno Territories, I don't know what else is out there. I'm not sure if any of us do."

Letting out a deep breath, Taryn opened the flap to their tent, Silia following her inside.

"Hopefully we find nothing at the coast. Hopefully the messages were wrong."

The next morning came too quickly for Taryn's sleep-deprived body. After the long march from their camp in Spectre Forest to the kingdom of Norithae, and the battle they'd found when they'd gotten there, she hadn't had much time to rest before being sent on the mission to the western edge of the continent. She stretched her long limbs and pulled her dark hair into a braid.

Leaving the tent after pulling a pair of leathers back on, she stepped out into the predawn morning to find most of the group already awake and eating around the fire. One of the Norithae warriors, Lars, smiled at her, handing her a piece of bread and dried meat. Taking it gladly, she lowered herself onto the log next to him, enjoying the warmth of the fire.

"Everyone is almost ready to fly out," he said, passing a mug of water to her as well. She glanced around, noticing most of the tents were put away and she regretted sleeping for so long.

"That's good. We should be able to make it to the edge of the forest today. We can camp under the cover of the trees again before heading out over the sea."

"Unless they've beat us there."

Although it was something Taryn didn't want to think about, she knew there was a possibility the invaders would already be on land by the time they made it to the coast. She just hoped that wouldn't be the case.

Having left the campsite shortly after breakfast, the group of ten warriors, following Taryn's lead, flew several more hours toward the western coast of Ekotoria. The sky was clear, giving them an unobstructed view of the ground, but giving anyone on the ground an unobstructed view of them as well. With the thick tree cover of Spectre Forest, she hadn't seen anyone, but that didn't mean no one was there. As they got closer to the edge of the landmass, the lush forest thinned, giving way to a more chaparral landscape. From their height in the air, she could just barely make out the sea and the sails of ships on the horizon.

Chapter 16

Aurelia

It had been two days since the warriors left Diapolis, Kason and Holera heading to Diapolis to meet with the king and the others scouting out the alleged ships sailing for their shores. Cristos had spent most of the past few days in council with the leaders from both militaries, while Aurelia spent a lot of her time training with Exie. If the war was coming, she needed to be prepared, and she knew Exie needed a distraction.

The air was warmer on the third day of waiting for news, Aurelia's tunic damp with sweat as she aimed her bow and fired an arrow at the target. Exie whooped, firing her own arrow and burying it in the target just beside Aurelia's. Aurelia sucked in a deep breath, the brine from the sea so similar to the air in Vaekros, the thought of her home filling her with a tinge of sadness. Until their recent battle with Warbotach, she'd had a piece of home with her. She and Septima had been there together, but now Septima was gone, and her absence was sometimes like a living weight on her shoulders. Kano was still with her, and she'd spent time with him every day, but he wasn't her sister.

"What are you thinking about?"

Exie asked as she held Aurelia's arrow in front of her. Aurelia hadn't even noticed her retrieve it.

Lowering herself to the ground, she set her bow and quiver by her side. Her friend sat beside her.

"I'm just thinking about home. Until Septima was taken, I hadn't missed home that much."

She shrugged, letting out a breath.

"Well, aside from our brother, but now that she's gone...it just makes me miss home a little bit more."

Exie nodded, patting Aurelia on the leg. "I miss her too. Did you see any new visions of her last night?"

Reluctantly shaking her head, Aurelia dug into the ground with her arrow, making random shapes in the dirt.

"I haven't had any visions in a couple of days. I wish I knew how to make the visions happen instead of them just coming out of nowhere."

"Well, you know what I think you should do. You need to talk to Variel. She seemed to know a lot about your heritage. Plus, she's an oracle. If anyone can help you hone your abilities, it would probably be her."

"I know, but even if I wanted to go to her, it's not safe. Cristos would never be okay with me leaving the protection of the city."

Exie shrugged, pulling out her water canteen and taking a sip. "If you can't go to Variel, why can't Cristos bring her here?"

The thought had never occurred to Aurelia. All she knew Variel left the city when Cristos' mother had been murdered and had remained in the forest behind protective wards ever since.

"I think it's more likely Variel wouldn't want to come back to the city, but I could bring it up to Cristos...see what he thinks."

Aurelia and Exie spent a little more time on the grounds, practicing archery and sparring, before Cristos found them later that day, after his meetings with the military leaders. Although Aurelia intended to speak to him about Variel, as Exie had suggested, she decided to wait until they'd settled down for the night. She was already drenched in sweat by the time he approached and Exie wandered off.

"Did you save any energy for me?" he asked as he pulled his sword from its sheath between his wings. "Or did Exie wear you out?"

Smirking, Aurelia scooped up her sword from where she'd laid it on the ground.

"I've always got energy for you."

Cristos swung before she was expecting it, but she met his blade with her own, the sound of metal against metal ringing out in the evening air. Letting out a chuckle, he stepped to the side to avoid her swing.

"Woah! You just keep getting better, my love. You almost took my leg off."

"I wasn't aiming for your leg."

Aurelia's response surprised even her, and she couldn't help but to snicker as Cristos' face fell in mock offense.

"You would've made our nights very quiet."

Tossing his sword to the ground, he rounded on her, scooping her into his arms, her blade clattering to the ground.

"And that would've been too bad. I'm rather fond of our nights."

Just as they were about to kiss, Exie ran back up to them, a look of urgency on her face.

"Blaedia needs to talk to both of you *now*. We just got a raven from Aegricia."

Aurelia's heart stilled in her chest and she pulled away from Cristos' arms without another word, following Exie as she ran toward the barracks. He didn't hesitate to follow behind. By the time they got into the barracks, several members of both militaries were already waiting around the table to hear the message.

The general tipped her head at them as they entered the room, her expression revealing nothing about what was held in the piece of paper in her hand. Slipping his arm around her waist, Cristos pulled Aurelia close as Blaedia handed him the message.

"A raven just found its way to us a little while ago...the first we've seen in a while."

Aurelia's chest tightened uncomfortably as she waited for him to unroll the letter and read it, hope and fear about news of her sister warring inside her. Sensing her anxiety, he squeezed her gently and opened the letter, holding it out so she could see it. The message was brief, but it was enough.

Septima is with Otera in the dungeon. They're safe for now.

Cristos read the letter out loud, the room silent as everyone hung on each word. Beside them, Exie slumped into a chair, breathing out an audible breath. Aurelia placed a hand on her shoulder.

Taking the letter back, Blaedia's eyes went distant for a moment before she seemed to snap back into the present.

"This is good. This is what we hoped for. They're together and Otera will protect her."

"So, what now?" Aurelia asked as she lowered herself into the chair next to her friend.

Moving behind her, Cristos placed a hand on her shoulder.

"We just have to wait until our warriors get back, so we know what we're up against. Until then, we need to focus on discovering how to get through Warbotach's protective shield around the city."

Blaedia nodded, slipping the note into her cloak pocket.

"I'll speak to my warriors with the warding gift and make a plan for a siege on the walls once we have backup. They'll have to start preserving their power now if there's any chance of us getting through."

Chapter 17

Kason

Waking the next morning, Kason and Holera ate breakfast in the tavern before setting off on foot for the ranch where they would get a horse for the remainder of their journey to Diapolis. The process had been quick, and the pair had set off on the back of an ebony steed named Moondancer before the sun made it to the highest point in the sky. After a half of a day riding on horseback, the giant gates, framed by magnificent statues, came into view as they arrived at the capital city of Embershell.

As had been the case on their first trip into Diapolis, the palace guards met them at the gate. Kason recognized one of them, the golden-haired Captain of the Guard, Kimo, who led the group, but it was the female on the horse with him that caught Kason by surprise.

"Calista?"

Holera's voice had been low, just loud enough for Kason to hear her. Grunting his acknowledgement, he urged their horse forward. The Aegrician healer lifted her hand in greeting as they moved through the massive city gates.

"His Majesty is expecting you at breakfast tomorrow," Kimo said, turning his horse to walk alongside them. "He knew you would need to rest from your travels."

Although Kason nodded, his jaw stiffened with annoyance. It was not unlike King Ailani to put off a meeting when it entailed discussions of an alliance.

"Time is of the essence, so if we could meet with—."

"That will not be possible," Kimo said, interrupting Kason before he'd even finished getting the words out. "King Ailani is not in the capital this evening. He will be back in the morning."

With the king not in the capital, there had been nothing Kason could have said to make the meeting happen any sooner. He was more than a little frustrated, but with nothing else to do, he and Holera retired to their guest room, cleaned up, and tried to rest from their long journey. Before leaving the foyer, they'd asked Calista to come to their room later that night so they could speak with her. They still didn't know why she'd never returned to the war camp with her people. There had been speculation that she was being held against her will, but she had not appeared distressed as she rode on Kimo's horse. If anything, she appeared content.

Thoughts of where King Ailani could possibly be plagued Kason as he ran Holera's bath, something he enjoyed doing for her when they had a tub to take advantage of. Having stayed in the war camp for the past many months, they'd been forced to use the showering tent for their nightly cleaning, aside from the times when Kason filled a copper trough with warm water, and had it brought into their tent.

Holera came into the bathing room as Kason turned off the tap wearing nothing more than a silk robe and Kason's mouth went dry. It didn't matter how many times he'd seen the curves of her breasts or the toned muscles of her stomach, she always brought him to his knees.

"Thank you for getting it ready for me," she said, fatigue clear in her voice. "You truly spoil me."

He grinned, getting to his feet and pulling her to his chest. "As I always will."

Just as Kason was getting out of the tub, his hair still dripping onto his shoulders, a knock sounded on the door to their suite. As Holera answered, Kason could see Calista's crimson hair from over her shoulder. His mate moved aside, allowing the Aegrician healer to pass.

Taking a few steps into the room, Calista closed the door behind herself, her face unreadable. Holera led her friend to the seating area where the two females sat on the luxurious emerald settee.

"I'm glad to see you're well, Calista. We were all worried about why you hadn't returned."

Pulling out three glasses from the hutch, Kason poured whiskey in each before setting two on the table in front of them.

The healer nodded, taking a sip from her glass.

"I was asked to stay here as an emissary as well as a guide if King Ailani chose to sail his military northward. I know messages were sent, but I admit I wasn't privy to what was contained in them."

Pulling out a chair, Kason sat beside his mate, who cleared her throat before speaking.

"And does the king plan to send his military northward?"

Calista glanced over her shoulder, looking at the closed door, before turning back to them.

"I haven't been privy to King Ailani's private meetings to discuss plans either, so I don't know much."

"Well, then, tell us what you do know."

Leaning back in her chair, Calista seemed to be thinking about Kason's request, but she didn't speak quickly, making him wonder what kind of secrets she'd been asked to keep. She may have been telling the truth about not knowing anything, but Kason wasn't so sure.

After a few silent minutes, Calista drained the rest of her whiskey and turned her eyes on Kason.

"I don't know if King Ailani plans to take his ships and dragons north, but I do know he's gone to the dragon's keep. That's where he is now. He left as soon as he received Blaedia's message about the ships heading toward our continent. If I had to guess, I'd suspect he's there to prepare his men and dragons for war."

Chapter 18

Otera

The sound of the metal hinges squealing pulled Otera from a deep sleep as she laid on one of the benches against the dungeon wall. Scrambling to her feet, she stood tall by the time the Warbotach guard sauntered in, the sneer on his face making him look even more menacing.

"Why are you here?"

Although Otera tried to fill her voice with authority, she realized she held none. The clenching inside her chest told her so.

"I see no food or water you've been sent to deliver."

Huffing something under his breath, he stepped forward, pulling manacles from around his back just as Septima opened her eyes, causing her to jolt upright. "I didn't come here for a delivery errand, *queen bitch*," he said, his voice more a growl than actual speech. "I came to get you and bring you to the king. He has need of you."

Otera's body stiffened, her heart beating in a panic. The last time she'd seen Uldon, he'd struck her, so she wasn't looking forward to seeing him again, not unless she could kill him.

"If the king needs to speak to me, then he should come here."

Closing the distance between them, the guard yanked Otera's arms forward, trapping them in the manacles. She struggled against them, but it was no use. Turning to look at Septima, the fear in the human's eyes turned Otera's stomach. If Uldon took her away, Septima would be alone. She'd promised to protect the human and she couldn't do that if she was gone.

Struggling against the manacles again as the guard held onto them, trying to drag her from the dungeon, flames burst from Otera's hands, sending the guard screaming as his flesh melted away in the heat. Using the temporary distraction, she slammed the iron manacles hard against the guard's head, knocking him unconscious.

"Hurry, Septima, get the key!"

With no hesitation, Septima rose from the bench, scurrying across the floor and grabbing the tiny copper key before placing it in the manacles. Otera sighed as the chains clanked to the floor and she immediately grabbed the guard's sword.

"If we're going to try to get away, we only have a few minutes to do so."

Eyes wide, Septima didn't speak for a moment and Otera had to shake her shoulders gently.

"Septima, do you want to try to escape?"

A hesitant nod was all she saw before pulling the shocked human toward the door.

"Then we need to go now!"

The injured guard had come to the cell alone, leaving the dungeon door wide open and the corridor empty. Otera held her finger up to her lips, telling Septima to remain silent as they snuck down the corridor. The sun had yet to shine through the small window of the palace's lower level, telling Otera it may have still been night. As they got to the end of the corridor leading into the servants' area, they stopped, Otera listening for voices through the door.

"If we can get through the servants' kitchen and out the back door, we can hide in the mountains and make our way around the city under the cover of darkness."

Otera's voice had been nothing more than a whisper but Septima nodded. Blowing out a deep breath, the queen nudged the door to the kitchen open just a few inches and peeked inside. To her surprise, a familiar set of silver eyes stared back at her from the sink. *Bremusa.*

The elemental's eyes went wide as she saw the queen and the human peering through the doorway of the kitchen and she abandoned what she was doing to dart across the room to them, pulling them inside.

"Your Highness, you're going to get caught. How did you get out?"

By the way Bremusa was scolding her at the same time as hugging her, she didn't know if her friend was angrier that she'd endangered herself or relieved she'd gotten out of the dungeon.

"Let's save that story for when we're somewhere safe. Is there a way to get us out of here?"

After a few moments of thinking, Bremusa pulled Otera across the room and into a closet where several uniforms and cloaks hung from hooks on the wall.

"Here. Change into these and tie your hair back."

"Do you have it, Bremusa?"

Otera knew she needed to flee while she could, but she couldn't do it without her crown, or at least without knowing it was safe and out of the hands of Uldon. Bremusa nodded, her lips falling into a fine line.

"It's with the Shadow Glass, Your Grace. He can't get to it."

Relieved, Otera dropped her dress to the floor and pulled on a servant's uniform. Septima did the same.

"Good. We need to get out of here before the guard wakes and realizes we're gone."

Bremusa grinned, and in a matter of moments, a beautiful onyx-haired woman stood where the elderly female had been only moments before.

Having never seen Bremusa shift before, Septima's jaw fell open and she sputtered for words.

"Bremusa's an elemental," Otera said as she fastened the guard's sword at her waist. "She can shift forms."

Seeming to snap out of her shock, Septima pulled the hood of her gray cloak over her head just as Bremusa nudged open the door, her own head covered by the hood of her black cloak.

"Traders are here to replenish the storage. If we can get into one of their wagons, they may be able to get us to port, or into the pass."

Sneaking out of the closet and back into the empty kitchen, the three women crept across the room to a door that led out into an alley behind the palace where deliveries were made.

Otera held the hilt of the sword in one hand and Septima's trembling hand in the other. Her heartbeat like a war drum in her ears, the danger of their situation not lost on her. Still, she knew they had to take the opportunity while they had it.

Pressing her shoulder to the door, Bremusa nudged it open, the chill of the night air fluttering Otera's cloak. As Bremusa suggested, there were four carts parked in front of the storage buildings at the back of the palace, their owners busy unloading goods and not looking in the direction of the back door.

Bremusa dipped her head before pushing the door open enough for them to walk through and out into the alley.

After so long in a dungeon, the scent of the briny water and the feel of the breeze against her face, made the backs of Otera's eyes burn, but she ignored the sensation, instead focusing on maintaining her newfound freedom.

Creeping forward through the shadows, they hid behind the wheel of the frontmost cart, waiting for the owner to unload the last of his product before slipping inside, the leather cover falling back in place as though they'd never disturbed it.

Chapter 19

Kason

Calista left shortly after telling them where the king had gone, but Kason was unable to get what she'd said out of his head. If what she suspected was true, and King Ailani was readying his troops, they would at least have a fighting chance of taking their kingdom back. He didn't want to get his hopes up, however. Until they'd spoken to the king himself, there was no way to know what his plans were.

When he and Holera woke the next morning in crisp sheets on a four-poster bed, his mind went directly to the looming war and the king's decision. Even the scent of his mate's skin couldn't stray his attention from the meeting they were to have that day. Their entire world rested on what King Ailani decided to do. Before they'd even had a chance to talk about what they would say to the king when they saw him, a servant knocked on the door to escort them to breakfast.

Taking a few minutes to get dressed, Kason and Holera left their guest quarters, following behind the servant down the corridor and into the dining room. After having visited the Diapolisian palace only weeks before, they could have found the room themselves, but didn't complain as she led the way.

By the time they'd stepped into the dining room, King Ailani and his consort, Makoa, were already seated at the table, cups of tea in their hands, carrying on a hushed conversation.

Their heads lifted as Kason and Holera entered, both of their faces spreading into smiles. The king may have been smiling with his mouth, but it didn't quite meet his eyes. A guard closed the door behind them as they took their seats at the table, Kason taking the chair closest to King Ailani.

"Welcome back, Kason. Holera," the king said, raising his mug as the servant set tea in front of each of them. "I hope your accommodations have been comfortable."

Raising his mug, Kason took a sip just as three servants returned, setting multiple dishes down in the center of the table.

"Your palace is beautiful, truly," Holera responded before Kason had a chance.

He grinned at her, taking her hand in his and kissing her knuckles.

"It's just as my mate said. I hope we can one day return to Embershell under better circumstances and have a chance to explore the city."

A more personable host than his husband, Makoa nodded, his smile genuine.

"We will have a great feast when the continent is no longer at risk."

Kason didn't want to read too much into Makoa's statement, but it had been hard not to.

"Although I appreciate your hospitality, Your Highness, my mate and I really should be getting back to Norithae. With the threat of invaders coming from another continent, no sword can be spared."

Setting his fork down on his plate, the king wiped his lips with a napkin.

"That is actually why I could not meet with you last night. I received a message from your general only hours before your arrival, speaking of ships being spotted off the coast of our continent. I felt it vital to send my own people to verify the claims."

Kason swallowed the lump in his throat.

"And have you made your decision?"

Taking a single glance at his consort, King Ailani returned his eyes to his guests across the table.

"I've realized that if I want the whole of the continent to remain free, and not be destroyed, I have no choice but to get involved."

Chapter 20

Aurelia

Although she'd seen it in her visions, having proof her sister was with the queen calmed some of Aurelia's worry. Septima was still in a dungeon, but she was alive, and she wasn't alone. Considering all the other possibilities, she realized Septima being in the Aegrician dungeon with Otera was the best-case scenario.

When she and Cristos retired to their suite that night, after sharing a dinner with the leaders of both militaries, it was with a lighter heart. They knew where Septima was, and they were going to rescue her.

Pulling off her boots, she let out a groan. Sparring with Exie, and then with Cristos, had her muscles tight and achy. If she was going to fight in another war, she knew she would have to work up her resistance.

Cristos grinned, handing her a glass of wine.

"Do you need me to rub those for you?"

Shaking her head, she pulled off her socks.

"I appreciate the offer, but I think what I really need right now is a bath and sleep. Today has been...a lot."

Kissing her on the top of the head, Cristos sauntered into the bathing room, the sound of water running meeting Aurelia's ears only a moment later. She smiled to herself, their conversation from the night before returning to her mind. He'd told her she was his bonded mate, a connection she'd suspected from the start, but having been raised in the human world, hadn't known for sure.

Standing and stretching out her limbs, she followed him.

Walking into the room and seeing Cristos leaning over the tub, running her bath, reminded Aurelia of when they'd first met and had escaped Norithae together, spending time at Variel's cottage while Exie healed. Even then, having only just met her, he'd warmed her water and run her baths.

It was just one of the things he'd always done for her without her ever having to ask.

He turned to look at her as she approached, a playful grin on his face as he rose to his full height and pulled her into a hug.

"We're going to get her back," he said as he kissed her, his lips lingering for a moment. "Soon."

Nodding against his chest, Aurelia listened to the steady beating of his heart.

"I know we will. I can feel it."

Squeezing her one more time, Cristos helped her remove her clothes before helping her into the tub and climbing in behind her. Sliding back between his legs, she leaned against his chest as he poured the warm water over her hair and shoulders. The sensation of the water cascading down her body relaxed her and soothed her aching muscles.

They laid there for a while, Cristos washing her hair and then her washing his, engaged in small talk that had nothing to do with a looming war. When they climbed into bed, wrapped in each other's arms as the fireplace flickered, it was with hope for the future.

The palace was relatively quiet when they woke the next morning. Aurelia and Cristos made their way down to the kitchen, taking a seat at the workbench just as the cook, Paulus, pulled a pan of rolls from the oven. The scent made Aurelia's mouth water.

The gray-haired male smiled at them as he turned around and saw them sitting in his kitchen, waiting to be fed.

"I could have sent your meal up to your rooms, Your Grace."

Setting the hot pan down on the wooden countertop, Paulus pulled the kettle off the fire and set it, along with two mugs and tea bags, down on the table in front of them.

Cristos grabbed the tea kettle, filling both their mugs.

"After all the time I've spent away, Paulus, it's just good to be back here with my people."

The cook dipped his chin before turning back to the stove and cracking eggs into a pan.

"We are glad to have you back, Your Grace. Breakfast will be ready in ten minutes if you and the lady are hungry."

Setting his mug down in front of him, Cristos cleared his throat.

"Paulus, when Warbotach was here, did you have a chance to interact with them much? Overhear their conversations?"

Aurelia stilled her breaths as they waited for a response. She wasn't sure what information Cristos was looking for with his inquiry, but she saw the disappointment on his face when Paulus shook his head.

"Most of the staff were allowed to remain in the palace and continue their chores, but the Warbotach invaders were careful to keep conversations of a sensitive kind away from the ears of their enemies. Aside from being instructed on what to cook, and where I could and could not venture, they didn't speak to me."

Clearing the disappointment from his expression, Cristos took a sip of his tea.

"And were you treated well, Paulus? You and the other servants?"

Paulus turned his back to them as he buttered the rolls and plated the rest of their breakfast.

"Warbotach may be a bunch of unsophisticated brutes, but they had no interest in angering the people tasked to cater to them. Plus," he said as he placed their plates down in front of them, filled with eggs, fried potatoes, and fresh buttered bread. "I don't think any of them wanted poison to end up in their porridge."

Aurelia snickered, her hand covering her mouth, so she didn't accidentally spit out her food. When Cristos turned to look at her, his eyes flickered with amusement.

"No, I guess they wouldn't have wanted that, although I do wish you would have done it anyway. Then we would've had a few less brutes to contend with moving forward."

"Aye," the older male said as he sat at the table across from them with his own plate of food. "I may not have rid the world of any Warbotach scum, but other citizens certainly did. They didn't all leave this city on the back of a horse, Your Grace." Chuckling, Paulus took a sip of his tea. "I believe Madame Sidonia at the Fearless Whisper Club down by the harbor rid the world of at least three."

Just thinking about a fierce brothel madam doing the work of a warrior and taking out their enemies sent Aurelia into a fit of giggles.

"I need to meet this female! What did she do to them?"

Cristos took a bite of his eggs, tipping his head for Paulus to answer the question.

"Madame Sidonia has very strict rules in her brothel, and if her workers feel threatened, they are allowed to defend themselves. The workers may not be trained warriors, but there are many potions kept on the premises that would knock a male out with one sip. Word has it that several Warbotach males found more in their glasses than whiskey."

"If her potion is that effective, we should get some batches of it made in case we need to use it for the war. Maybe we can find a way to get it into the Warbotach camps."

The words left Cristos' mouth just as she'd had the same thought.

"Exie and I could go and talk to her today, while you meet with Blaedia and the others."

Taking the last bite of his breakfast, Cristos nodded.

"I think that's a great idea. It'll give you a chance to meet your people, and for them to meet you, since you will be their queen before too long."

Chapter 21

Taryn

The armada sailing toward the Ekotorian coast chilled Taryn's fiery phoenix blood. There were more than just ships coming for them. There were dragons. Three of them. With less than a dozen warriors with her, there was nothing they could do to stop the invaders from coming ashore. At that moment, they were utterly helpless.

Letting out a signal call, the commander circled back over the forest, landing in a clearing before they could be sighted. She shifted quickly, leaning over with her hands on her knees as she tried to catch her breath. Her heart pounded painfully against her ribcage, fear that only came with the threat of war filling her.

The other warriors landed one-by-one at her side, Lars immediately starting to pace as the phoenixes shifted into their fae forms.

"We are so fucked," he said, his wings tucking in tightly against his back. "We have to get back to Norithae and warn everyone. Maybe evacuate the cities."

Taryn's mind went straight to Kason and Holera, wondering if they'd met with the king of Diapolis yet. She wondered if his military was gearing up to join their fight in the north at that very moment. Even if he did send his warriors and dragons, the cities would still have not been safe for their civilian population. If there was a risk of the cities burning to ashes, they needed to get the children and those incapable of fighting somewhere safe.

Straightening her back, Taryn scanned the troubled faces of the warriors around her. No matter how brave they were, none of them were a match for a full-grown fire-breathing dragon. It would take many warriors to fight even one, and their invaders had three. She didn't know how many dragons King Ailani had, but she hoped it was more.

"Lars is right. Even if King Ailani is sending his dragons and ships full of warriors along our eastern shore right now, the cities are no place for our civilians. We need to go back and evacuate. We need to bring those who can't fight into the mountains and away from the coast. They will need camps set up and wards to shield them."

"Who could be leading this?" one of the Norithaean warriors asked, a yellow-haired male that Taryn had yet to get to know. "Who would have something to gain by supporting Warbotach?"

Taryn stiffened, the words leaving her mouth before she'd even finished processing the thought.

"Can you think of no one?"

The sound of Lars' steps halted as he turned to face her.

"The exiled queen. *Joneira.*"

Chapter 22

Septima

The wheels of the produce cart squealed as the driver edged the horses to take it forward. Septima's nails dug into Otera's hand but the queen didn't seem to mind. Not knowing where the driver was headed, all they could do was hope he took them out of Warbotach-held Aegricia before the guards realized they were gone. They maintained their silence, the three of them huddled together, the bumpy road putting Septima to sleep.

Rubbing the sleep from her eyes, Septima awoke just as the sound of the horses' steps slowed, the cart rolling to a stop as they sat quietly inside. Septima held her breath, hoping the merchant intended to head to bed and not to reload his cart. She didn't know where they were, but it was clear they hadn't simply traveled to the Aegrician harbor to board a ship. They'd been traveling for long enough to have been out of the city completely, however. That, in itself, was a relief.

A sliver of sunlight beamed in through a slit in the cart's cover as they listened to the driver disconnect his horses, his steps fading into the distance.

"We should go now," Bremusa said, pulling the cover aside to peer outside. "It's a farm. We're somewhere in the valley between Aegricia and Norithae."

A flutter of excitement filled Septima's chest.

"My sister is in Norithae with the Aegrician military. We need to get there."

Bremusa nodded, peering outside again.

"Once we get out of here, I can shift, and we can get to Norithae before nightfall."

A few moments later, the dark-haired elemental slid through the opening in the cover, her boots silent as they hit the ground.

Sucking in a breath, Septima scooted to the edge of the cart, dropping to her feet and then stepping out of the way so Otera could climb out behind her.

Rocky cliffs ran along the back of the property, but the farm was extensive, fields of crops stretching as far as she could see. The merchant was nowhere in sight, having left the cart parked on the side of a large wooden barn to stable his horses. Chickens searched the grounds for bugs, scurrying away as the three females stepped toward them.

Septima wasn't familiar with the landscape of the northern part of the continent, but the view took her breath away. The mountains were massive, snow still dusting their peaks although the winter would give way to spring before long.

Motioning for them to follow her, Bremusa crept behind the barn, shifting with a flair of fire, leaving a large golden phoenix where the female had been only moments before.

With no time to spare, Septima climbed onto the large phoenix's back, Otera saddling in behind her, and Bremusa's great golden wings flapped, lifting them off the ground and into the sky.

Chapter 23

Kason

With the alliance they'd gone to Diapolis to achieve, Kason and Holera set off toward Norithae by air with a fleet of ships at their backs. The envoy King Ailani had sent to the western coast had yet to return, but the accounts were undeniable. The continent was under attack, and from more than just Warbotach.

Kason and Holera had met with Calista briefly before leaving Embershell, discovering there was more to her remaining in the southern kingdom than just as assurance. She and the Captain of the Guard, Kimo, had become mated. Once the war was over, she intended to make Embershell her home.

Knowing people were still finding joy in their lives and planning for their futures filled Kason with hope for his own life with Holera. Maybe, once their kingdom was free, they could return to the cabin in the mountains and have a family.

Unable to make the entire journey from Diapolis to Norithae in one stretch, the couple returned to the tavern in the town of Claywind. Taking a table in the back of the room, Kason ordered whiskey and dinner, as well as a room for the night. Instead of sitting across the table from his mate, Kason pulled his chair right next to her, wrapping his arm around her shoulder and pulling her close. The need to be close to her, to touch her, was palpable.

"I'm tired," Holera said as she snuggled into his side. "I'm so ready to crawl into bed after we eat."

Kissing her on the forehead, Kason nodded.

"I think we will both pass out the moment our heads hit the pillow."

The server returned with their meal a moment later, and they ate quickly, ready to retire for the night. The morning would come early and bring with it another long journey. Once they returned to Norithae, war would follow, and rest would be difficult to come by.

Without the worry of whether King Ailani would assist in the war or not, there was much less weight on Kason and Holera's shoulders to keep them up that night. Holding his mate in his arms, Kason caressed Holera's back until she fell asleep.

Sparing only enough time to eat breakfast the next morning, Kason and Holera left the town of Claywind by air, flying north for Norithae. Once over the Elder Sea, they could see King Ailani's fleet in the distance, sailing northward on the water, as they soared through the clouds. With his dragons escorting his ships, Holera circled around, choosing to fly over the forest instead. Although they were King Ailani's allies, they didn't want to take the chance of getting in the way of an angry dragon.

They landed in Norithae at least a day ahead of when Diapolis' ships would make port, giving them time to catch everyone up on what was to come. As late as it was, there were not many people still awake on the palace grounds, aside from the guards who were on duty. Kason and Holera aimed directly for the barracks, knowing the general would want them to meet with her right away, but a call sounded just as they crossed the grounds. A phoenix was approaching them from the north, from the direction of Aegricia.

Chapter 24

Septima

Bremusa's golden wings carried the two escaped prisoners further from the dungeon that had held them with every beat. Holding firmly onto the reins, Septima watched as the kingdom of Aegricia passed in the distance, the sun moving across the sky and finally going into its slumber by the time they'd reached the kingdom of Norithae.

Flying over Norithae had been a surreal experience after having been carted into the kingdom as a prisoner and marching into the kingdom as a soldier. She'd never seen it from the air, never seen the majestic view of the palace, with its towers and dark granite walls, or how the sea crashed against the cliffs. The moonlight reflected off the water and hundreds of fires burned in the windows of the palace and across its grounds, making the scene appear magical.

Although she didn't know what kinds of wards were protecting the capital city, excitement still filled her. She and Otera were free at least, and she would be reunited with her sister and her mate soon.

Over the past few days, she'd been trying not to think about Exie so she wouldn't have to let in the pain of missing her, and the worry of never seeing her again. Missing Aurelia had been hard enough. Now that they were about to be reunited, the emotions that filled her were powerful and burned at the backs of her eyes.

Touching down on the street outside the palace gates, Septima and Otera climbed off Bremusa's back, the elemental shifting back into her fae form quickly. It only took a moment for the gates to open, and for no less than a dozen guards to come running out, swords in their hands. Otera lowered her cloak, stepping forward into the flickering light of the guards' torches, a collective gasp echoing through the space as they recognized the Aegrician queen. She was clearly the last person they'd expected to see in their streets.

The guards parted as two figures moved past, barreling to the front of the group. Blaedia broke through the crowd first, freezing in place as Exie fell to her knees beside them. With a burst of emotion, Septima darted past and dropped beside her lover, pulling Exie in her arms.

Exie's shoulders shook as she sobbed, running her hands up Septima's back and down her arms.

"Are you okay? Did they hurt you?"

Pulling away just enough to study her face, Exie cupped Septima's cheeks with her hands, her eyes welling with emotion as she leaned forward and kissed her.

"I was so worried about you. I was so worried."

Exie pulled Septima to her chest again, burying her face in Septima's neck. Stroking Exie's hair, Septima leaned back and looked into her lover's honey-colored eyes again.

"I'm here, and I'm not hurt. It's going to be okay."

As Exie and Septima held each other outside the palace gates, Otera and Blaedia were in each other's arms as well. So wrapped up in her own reunion, Septima had nearly forgotten how long Otera had been away from her mate, but seeing them hold each other, she knew their love for each other was strong. There was no doubt Blaedia would see Otera through her recovery from captivity.

The sound of boots caught Septima's attention and she turned toward the group of guards to see Kason and Holera running out through the palace gates. Holera's hands went over her mouth as her steps slowed, shock on her face as she took in the sight of her queen and then turned to look at Septima.

Taking his mate by the hand, Kason approached Blaedia and the queen, bowing from the waist.

"King Ailani's fleet will be here by morning and the invaders are nearing the continent's western shores. We will need to evacuate the cities and prepare for an attack."

Blaedia stiffened, tucking Otera further into her side.

"Then we must get Septima and Otera inside so they can eat and rest, and we must wake Cristos."

Chapter 25

Aurelia

The sound of someone pounding on the bedchamber startled Aurelia out of a deep sleep. Cristos mumbled something before rolling out of bed and shuffling to the door. Sliding out of bed, Aurelia slipped her cloak over her nightdress, heading to the door just as a few excited words met her ear when the servant spoke to her mate.

"The queen is here."

Forgetting about her shoes altogether, she rushed past Cristos and the servant, her heart pounding as she followed the sound of voices. Cristos chased after her, his heavy footsteps echoing through the corridor, but she didn't slow down for him to catch up. Just as she turned the corner into the palace foyer, her steps faltered as her knees threatened to collapse from beneath her. Standing in the entrance, safe and holding onto Exie, was her sister.

"Sissy!" her sister cried out when their eyes met, Septima leaving Exie's side and closing the space between them, wrapping her arms around Aurelia. Aurelia's body sagged against her little sister, disbelief and joy warring inside her.

Pulling away to look into her sister's face, the first of Aurelia's tears fell.

"I don't understand. How did you escape? How did you get here?"

The smile that spread across Septima's face expanded Aurelia's heart. Septima's eyes flicked over Aurelia's shoulder before looking back at her.

"I'm here thanks to your aunt."

Words stuttering out of her, Aurelia turned in the direction Septima was looking, her mouth falling open as she gazed at the face that looked so much like her mother.

To Aurelia's surprise, the queen was wrapped in Blaedia's arms. She hadn't even known that Blaedia had a lover or a mate, much less that she'd been in a relationship with the queen. The general had always kept her personal life private, at least in the conversations they'd had. Suddenly, the emotion Aurelia had glimpsed in the general's eyes as they'd discussed Otera previously made sense.

Catching her stare, a flash of recognition showed in the queen's eyes and she took a hesitant step toward her niece. Aurelia turned to her sister, who still stood by her side, their fingers interlaced.

"Does she know who I am?"

Septima shook her head, but the side of her mouth lifted in a smile.

"No. I didn't want to say anything where Warbotach could overhear, but you look just like her, so I think she just figured it out."

When Aurelia turned back around, her aunt had moved several steps closer. Aurelia shrugged, unsure what to say. Before she could utter a word, a female with onyx hair and quicksilver eyes approached her, her expression in complete awe.

The female reached out, cupping Aurelia's cheek with her hand.

"You look so much like your mother. Messalina and I were close friends."

Turning to Otera, the dark-haired female motioned the queen forward.

"Come, Your Majesty. Meet your niece: the queen who was promised all those years ago."

A loving hand settled on the small of Aurelia's back as Cristos moved closer to her, showing support if she needed it. With everything going on, she'd nearly forgotten he was there.

Septima's hand grounding her, Aurelia watched as the queen approached with a look of confusion on her face. Just like Aurelia, Otera's hair hung in long crimson locks, but the color had dulled with the many months she'd spent in the dungeon.

"Are you Messalina's daughter?"

Although her expression was cautious, Otera's tone sounded hopeful.

"It can't be true. How? How is this possible?"

Before Aurelia could respond, the palace doors swung open and Kason and Holera walked in, followed by Taryn and the group of warriors that had been sent across the continent a few days earlier. The look on Taryn's face twisted Aurelia's stomach. It was clear whatever news she had to share, it wasn't good news.

Cristos, recognizing the importance of whatever they needed to discuss, waved the group toward the dining room.

"Come, let's all go sit down so we can talk. I think everyone could use a glass of whiskey."

By the time they'd all piled into the large palace dining room, every available chair had been taken. Two servants passed around glasses of whiskey while another two headed to the kitchens to prepare food. With the queen, Bremusa, and Septima having just escaped from the dungeon, and the warriors having flown from across the continent, there were many hungry mouths to feed. Aurelia sat between Cristos and her sister, the queen and general on his other side.

Taking a sip of her whiskey, Taryn cleared her throat, drawing their attention.

"We need to evacuate the city. There are more than just ships heading toward our shores. There are dragons."

Heart dropping into her stomach, Aurelia set her glass down on the table, unsure how to process what she'd just heard.

"I thought the only dragons left were in Diapolis."

"On the continent, yes, but I'm not sure if any of us know what lives outside of Ekotoria," Cristos said, tapping his finger on the side of his glass. "Do we know where they're coming from, Taryn? Any indication from what you saw?"

The commander shook her head, turning her eyes to one of the Norithae warriors who sat near her. Their eyes shared unspoken words as the servants set plates of meat, cheese, and fruit along the center of the table. Once the servants left the room, Taryn returned her attention to Cristos.

"We didn't get close enough to see the flags on the ships," she said, "but they're sailing with three full-grown dragons. We flew back straight away so we could evacuate the city before they got here. We need to get the civilians away from the coast."

Tension in Cristos' face was undeniable, his eyebrows furrowed as he scratched the stubble on his chin.

"We will need to send out warriors tonight to set up a camp in the valley and ward it."

The warrior beside Taryn stood.

"I'll go to the barracks now and pull together a group to start gathering supplies."

Cristos nodded and turned to Kason as the warrior left the room, Taryn following him.

"What happened in Diapolis? Did King Ailani agree to assist us?"

With everything that had transpired since she'd been awoken in the middle of the night by banging on their bedchamber door, she'd forgotten all about how Kason and Holera had just returned from the southern kingdom.

"King Ailani's fleet is on the way here as we speak," Kason said as he set his whiskey on the table. "He'd heard about the threat to our western coast, not only from Blaedia's letter but from his own people too. He did not say which way he'd been leaning before he learned of the foreign threat, but he did admit it was the deciding factor in his decision to send aid."

Aurelia's chest squeezed uncomfortably as Kason spoke, not from fear, but from what it meant that the Diapolisian fleet would be arriving on their shores the following day. War was upon them and there was nothing they could do to stop it. They'd known it was an eventuality for months, had even fought in a battle when entering Norithae, but a full-scale war had been avoided up until that point. Once the Diapolisian warriors and dragons arrived on their shores, war would follow shortly thereafter, and Aurelia knew she wasn't ready. If she was being honest with herself, she didn't think she could fight at all.

Some of the tension in Cristos' face seemed to relax a little, but just as he was about to respond to Kason, Otera leaned forward in her chair, fire blazing in her eyes.

"I don't know whose armada she's commanding, but there is no doubt who is leading the charge toward our shores."

Shifting in her chair, Otera's hands dug into the armrests.

"Joneira means to take Aegricia again."

"Joneira?"

Cristos' voice was laced with incredulity.

"The exiled queen? You think *she's* behind this? That she's supporting Warbotach's bid to take over the human lands?"

Otera nodded, draining the rest of her whiskey.

"I think they made a deal. I think Warbotach agreed to help her take back Aegricia and that she would bring allies to help them take over the human lands."

Dread burning in her throat, Aurelia tried to swallow it back.

"Do you think they would try to bring their dragons through the portal? Humans have no way to fight something so destructive."

Septima's hand slid into Aurelia's, the touch providing some comfort. The queen's mouth fell into a thin line as she turned her eyes to Bremusa, the female dipping her head in the smallest of nods. When Otera turned back to look at her niece, something flashed behind her eyes that Aurelia couldn't decipher.

"We won't let that happen, even if we have to destroy the portal itself."

"Destroy the portal," Cristos said, the words sounding more like a question. "Is that even possible? It's been there as long as the kingdoms themselves."

The thought had never occurred to Aurelia. She squeezed her sister's hand, waiting for the queen to explain but it was her dark-haired friend who spoke.

"The portal is connected to the Aegrician crown. If I destroy the crown, the portal will be destroyed as well."

"But if the portal is destroyed, that means I could never return to the human lands. Septima and I would never be able to see our father or brother again."

When they'd first been taken in by the Aegrician warriors, Exie had warned them that they'd never be able to return to Vaekros once they'd left, but Aurelia had never considered the finality of it. She always knew in the back of her mind that the portal was there just in case she needed to go home.

"If Bremusa destroys my crown," Otera said, glancing toward her friend again, as though she were looking for confirmation. "The Ekotorian portal will be destroyed, but there are undoubtedly other portals in our world. I'm not sure where they are, but there are stories of them existing in far-away places."

Resting his elbows on the table, Cristos tapped his finger on his glass, his eyes scanning the faces in the room.

"If we destroy this portal, it's safe to say Warbotach would just go looking for another way into the human lands."

Otera nodded, lifting her glass for the servant to fill it.

"That's why we need to destroy them once and for all."

Chapter 26

Otera

O nce the plans for evacuating the city were in place, Otera was set up in a bedchamber in the palace. Although Blaedia was hesitant to stay apart from her warriors, she returned to the barracks to get her belongings before returning to the suite with her mate.

Otera sat for a moment on the chair in front of the fire, taking in the beauty of the room and breathing deeply. She was free after months of living in a dungeon, and she didn't know how exactly to process it.

Exhaustion pulled her to the bathing room, along with the fact that she hadn't had a good bath in longer than she could remember.

Turning on the tap, she watched as the steam rose from the water. The door to the bedchamber clicked open and Otera recognized Blaedia's footsteps right away, the sound of them filling her heart with warmth.

She'd missed her mate more than she wanted to admit, and now that they'd been reunited, she didn't even know what to do. It had been so long since they'd touched, since she'd been touched by anyone aside from being manhandled by the Warbotach beasts.

Dropping her bag on the ground, a grin spread across Blaedia's face as she saw Otera sitting by the tub, and she crossed the room quickly before scooping the queen up in her arms.

"I've missed you," Blaedia said as she nuzzled into Otera's neck. "Let's get you into the tub. I know you must be looking forward to it after all you've been through."

Pulling back enough to look into Blaedia's silver eyes, Otera grinned before pulling her mate's mouth to hers, kissing her deeply. The taste of her and the feel of Blaedia's tongue caressing hers, pulled a groan from the queen's throat.

"It's not the only thing I've been looking forward to."

"Is that so?"

Blaedia spoke against Otera's neck before kissing the flesh there.

"There are many things I missed, so let's get you in the tub, and I can show you. We have a lot of time to make up for."

With no more convincing, Otera unlaced her tunic, tossing it to the ground before reaching forward, pulling on the clasps of Blaedia's leathers.

"Will you join me?"

Leaning forward, Blaedia kissed her again, nibbling on Otera's lower lip as she unbuckled Otera's trousers. When they dropped like a puddle at her feet, she wrapped her arms around her lover, backing her toward the tub and guiding her inside.

Blaedia slid into the tub behind her mate, pulling her between her thighs. Otera leaned back against her lover's chest, trailing her fingers up and down Blaedia's thigh. Warm water cascaded over her body as Blaedia poured water over her with a glass.

"Would you like me to wash your hair, my fires?"

The feeling of the warm water sliding down her body, and Blaedia's soft skin against hers, brought back feelings Otera hadn't allowed in since she'd been forced into the dungeon. She was incredibly aroused and would have allowed Blaedia to do anything to her at that moment.

"I would love for you to wash my hair, and then I want to get out of the tub so I can thank you properly."

Blaedia leaned forward, kissing Otera on her neck as she slid her hand up Otera's stomach and squeezed her breast gently.

"Then let me get you clean so I can take you to bed. It's been a long time and I don't think I can handle waiting much longer."

Sliding into bed with Blaedia for the first time since before she'd been thrown in the dungeon, Otera crawled on top of her mate, straddling Blaedia's waist. The candlelight flickered, illuminating her mate's exotic beauty, her up tilted eyes the color of melted silver, her skin that always looked sun kissed, and the deep onyx of her silky hair.

"You're so beautiful like this," she said as she caressed her hands down Blaedia's perfect breasts.

Her lover's eyes swirled with desire as she looked at her, stroking her hand through Otera's long crimson waves before moving her attention down to Otera's breast, taking her hardened nipple into her mouth.

"You're just as beautiful as the day I met you, my fires."

Leaning forward, Otera pulled Blaedia's mouth to hers, grinding against her mate's body between her thighs. The friction was delicious, but she needed more. After so long without release, she needed it.

Always perceptive to her needs, Blaedia flipped them over, settling between Otera's thighs as she laid on her back. The first swipe of her mate's tongue through her folds sent a stroke of lightning through Otera's body. It had been so long since she'd been touched in such a way, so every sensation was magnified.

As Otera thrusted her fingers into her lover's hair, Blaedia licked her cunt again, closing her mouth around the sensitive bundle of nerves and sucking as she slid two fingers inside.

Desperate for release, Otera moaned, writhing beneath Blaedia and stroking her back with her foot. Every thrust of Blaedia's fingers inside her had her body winding tighter and tighter, the sounds coming from Otera's mouth loud and raw, although she tried to muffle them with a pillow.

When the intensity of her mate's mouth on her cunt increased, Otera's release crashed into her, Blaedia's name on her lips as her thighs squeezed around her head.

Otera collapsed on the bed, satiated and spent, with her mate in her arms. She only took a moment to recover before rolling her mate over again, intending to give to Blaedia just as much pleasure as her mate had just given to her. She may have been tired, but they had a lot of lost time to catch up on.

Chapter 27

Aurelia

Although she wanted to spend time with her sister, having just gotten her back, Septima had Exie now, and Aurelia knew she was exhausted. So, while Septima and Exie followed the servant to the guest chambers set up for them, Aurelia went with Cristos to the barracks as the warriors readied to leave for the mountains. With the Diapolis fleet arriving within the next day, the city needed to be evacuated of those citizens who were unable to fight. They hoped the city would survive the war, but there was no guarantee it would not be turned to cinders with dragons fighting on both sides.

By the time they got into the barracks meeting room, Lars had already gathered a group of warriors from both sides, as well as supplies to take to the location of the camp. Aurelia didn't know much about the landscape of the northern part of the continent, but Cristos instructed them to find a place within the valley to set up camp, somewhere safely away from any large settlements that may be targeted by their foreign invaders.

Although Taryn and Lars had intended to join the flyers in looking for a location for the camp, Cristos chose Faidon to lead the group since Taryn and Lars had just returned from the journey across the continent. With war looming, it was clear Cristos wanted the soldiers to have a chance to rest before they'd be needed to fight. Aurelia admired his consideration for his soldiers. He'd doubted his ability to be king from the start, but she didn't think there was even one other person who didn't respect and believe in him.

Once the group of warriors left, loaded with supplies, she and Cristos returned to their bedchamber to get a few more hours of sleep.

As soon as the door shut behind them, Cristos turned to her and pulled her into his arms.

"I promised we would get her back, but I hadn't expected her to free herself."

Smiling against his chest, Aurelia nodded. She closed her eyes, indulging for a moment in the feeling of his heart beating against her chest.

"I still can't believe it's real. I can't believe she's back and she's safe."

Caressing her back, Cristos kissed her on the forehead.

"Hopefully knowing she's safely tucked into bed in the palace will help you to sleep better tonight. Although I know what's ahead is enough to keep you awake."

Pulling away, she looked into his brilliant blue eyes. Even with several days' worth of stubble on his face and hair that needed a trim, he was the most handsome man she'd ever seen.

"I'm certainly not ready for a war, but I don't think any of us are."

Cristos nodded, kissing her deeply. Eyes falling closed, she wrapped her arms around his back, caressing the base of his wings. He groaned as his tongue caressed hers, lifting her into his arms and carrying her to the bed. Laying her gently on the silken sheets, he crawled over her, settling between her thighs.

"You can never truly be ready for war, but I'm not going to let anything happen to you. I told you that when we sat on Variel's roof, and nothing has changed since then."

Aurelia knew they needed sleep, but at that moment she didn't care. Her sister being safe gave her the permission she needed to enjoy herself without the sting of guilt. She didn't know what the next several days would bring, which was a feeling she was experiencing more and more, but her relationship with Cristos was something she could always depend on.

When Aurelia awoke the next morning, the bed beside her was empty, but the sheets were still warm. Her mate had woken, but he hadn't been gone long. Stretching her limbs and yawning, she tossed the blankets off and climbed out of bed. If he wasn't in their suite, then she expected to find him in the kitchens or in the barracks. Going into the bathing room, she cleaned her face and her teeth and pulled on a tunic and trousers, lacing up her boots before leaving their chambers. Before she even made it to the door of the kitchen, voices met her ears.

Opening the kitchen door, pure joy hit Aurelia when she saw her family sitting at the large prep table, talking as they sipped tea. Cristos, Septima, and Exie all turned to face her as she walked in, her sister jumping up from the table and running forward to embrace her. The many braids Septima had worn for years had been replaced by a single plait down her back. Aurelia pulled away to look into her sister's face. Septima looked vibrant and happy, beautiful as always.

"We didn't want to wake you, sissy. Are you hungry? Paulus is making a big breakfast for us."

Aurelia smiled so wide it nearly hurt as she followed her sister to the table. Choosing a chair between Septima and Cristos, her mate leaned over to kiss her as soon as she sat.

"Warriors flew down the coast this morning and reported that King Ailani's fleet will be here in a few hours," he said, pouring her a mug of tea. "We've sent another group toward the western side of the continent to get a better idea of the location of the invaders."

"You've certainly been busy this morning."

She hadn't thought Cristos had been awake for long, but by the list of things he'd already accomplished that morning, she realized he must have left their bed hours before she woke.

"Has the evacuation started?"

Cristos nodded.

"Those who couldn't fly themselves were either carried, traveled on horseback, or by wagon. The camp is set up in the valley to the west. It's many miles away from both king-doms and the coast so the area should be safe from attack. Wards have been set up just in case, and enough supplies were brought to sustain the people for weeks. We've ordered a small regiment of soldiers to remain there, as well as a healer. They should be safe in the camp until this is over."

Just hearing about all the preparations that were in place, especially those to keep the civilians safe, settled some of the anxiety that had been plaguing Aurelia ever since they'd first marched toward Norithae.

The door to the kitchen opened and Blaedia and Otera walked in just as Paulus started to set plates of food down on the table in front of them. There was evidence of Otera's months in the dungeon, her body still showing signs of hav-ing been underfed, but the queen looked clean and well-rest-ed. It would take time for her to return to the female she once was but being back with her mate would allow her to recover.

Walking hand in hand, Blaedia led Otera to the table, pulling out the chair for her to sit, before sitting beside her. The smile on her aunt's face warmed Aurelia's heart. She'd never known that Otera had a mate waiting for her when she escaped the dungeon, so knowing she had someone who loved her and would take care of her meant a lot to Aurelia.

Once everyone had a plate in front of them, Paulus left the room, leaving the six of them to eat and talk in private.

Septima had not exaggerated when she'd said the cook had created a big breakfast for them and the smells wafting in the air in front of her made her mouth water. Not only did the plate have eggs and toast, but he'd also fried pieces of ham for them and sliced fresh apples. Stomach growling as she took her first bite, Aurelia closed her eyes when the flavors hit her tongue, smiling as her family, both blood and found, talked with one another as they enjoyed their meal.

Chapter 27

Taryn

Although Cristos asked Taryn, Lars, and the rest of the group who'd traveled to the western coast to stay behind when the first fighters sought out a site to set up camp for the evacuees, she and Lars chose to fly out the next morning to transport those who couldn't fly themselves.

Setting out at first light, Taryn flew with a mother and child on her back toward the western part of the valley. Lars flew at her side, carrying the mother's other child.

In her phoenix form, she couldn't converse with the winged male at her side, or those riding on her back. She kept her eyes facing forward, flapping her great crimson and black wings in a steady rhythm, taking them just below the clouds. The journey was only supposed to take them a few hours, if the threatening storm didn't delay them. Cristos expected them to return to Windreach that evening, so she hoped the storm would hold off.

By the time they got to the camp, however, the thought of returning to the city was dashed. Although winter was coming to an end, it seemed to want to hold on as long as it could, and the freezing rain that pelted Taryn as she shifted back into her fae form was proof of that.

Securing her hood over her head, she led the mother and children into the dinner tent, Lars entering behind them.

"Is there anyone here who can reinforce the wards? Hold off the weather a bit longer?"

Lars shook his head, moving toward an empty table and sitting down. One of the cooks approached them, dropping off mugs of hot tea and plates of meaty stew. The scent made Taryn's mouth water, so she wasted no time taking a bite while waiting for Lars to respond.

"Most of the warriors who can ward have returned to Windreach toward the city. Since they intend to hold the wards steady in case of attack, they had to go back."

Although Taryn understood the reason why they'd left, the camp would be incredibly uncomfortable without a way to block out the storm. Everyone would need to stay in their shelters.

"Is there enough firewood?"

If there wasn't, she knew it would be difficult to find dry firewood since the rain had already started.

"We should have enough. A group went to Spectre Forest early in the day to get more. They have a shelter to keep it dry and I believe all the tents are stocked. Once these people finish eating, we just need to get them into tents for the night and hope the storm doesn't get any worse."

Frigid wind blew through the space as another Norithaean warrior escorted an elderly couple into the dining tent. They sat at a table near the fire, the cook immediately bringing them mugs of hot tea and plates of dinner. She watched them for a moment, grateful they'd been brought somewhere out of harm's way before the city was attacked.

Thoughts of her mate flooded into her mind, squeezing the ache that had been in her chest since the day she and the warriors had been forced to flee their kingdom. It had been months since she'd seen Cassius, and with no ability to contact him, she had no way to know if he was okay, or if he was even still alive. Not knowing ate away at her, pushed her to focus solely on her training and the war. Being captured by Warbotach weeks earlier and forced into the dungeon had nearly broken her, but the hope of seeing him again had pulled her out of the dark place she'd fallen into. She couldn't lie to herself, however. Going so long without the touch of a male and being around such handsome warriors in Norithae had been more than tempting.

When she turned her attention back to Lars, she pulled the image of Cassius' handsome face back to the forefront of her mind, hoping her willpower would not break. Her survival in the war was not guaranteed, and if she would die in the days to come, she didn't want to spend the rest of her time alone.

Finishing the last of her stew, Taryn stood, turning a glance toward the exit.

"If we aren't going back to the capital until after the storm, I guess I should turn in and try to get a few hours of sleep. I'd imagine there are tents for us?"

Lars nodded, standing as well.

"There are. Come. We can ask the cooks which ones are available."

Chapter 28

Septima

The storm hit just as the Diapolisian fleet entered the Norithaean harbor. Warriors were sent down to help secure the ships, but the dragons, six in all, had continued into the mountains, undoubtedly, to look for shelter. Septima followed Exie into the palace meeting room, taking a seat around the perimeter of the room as the military leaders of the three kingdoms filed into the room, followed by both kings and the queen.

After everything they'd shared in the dungeon and on their escape, Septima wondered how the queen was feeling now that she was back in the arms of her mate, free at last. From the brightness in Otera's eyes and the flush of her cheeks, Septima believed the queen would truly recover from her ordeal. The war was weighing on all of them, but they also all had reasons to be hopeful. With the arrival of King Ailani from Diapolis, they had a chance to win the war.

Dressed in a gold-embroidered violet tunic with well-fitted black trousers, the king of Diapolis did not look like what Septima had imagined. His hair was the same golden color as Exie's and hung in loose curls past his shoulders and his turquoise-colored eyes didn't show the same sleep deprivation that the rest of them did. He entered the room hand-in-hand with his consort, a handsome male dressed to sail into battle, and sat near the head of the table, just to the right of Cristos and directly across from Otera and Blaedia. Servants entered quickly, pouring glasses of whiskey for everyone in the room. Septima took hers gladly, enjoying the burn of the liquid as it hit her throat.

Reaching across the table, Cristos shook King Ailani's hand, dipping his head to the king's husband.

"I can't tell you how much we appreciate you being here to aid in this fight. I understand why you were hesitant."

King Ailani nodded, taking a sip of his whiskey.

"My spies came back from the western sea speaking of ships and dragons from the Inferno Territories. If Uldon is bringing in allies from off the continent, those with many ships and dragons, there is more he wants than to simply cross the portal."

"He's conquering the continent for Joneira," Bremusa interrupted. "When she was forced out of Aegricia after she'd taken the throne by force, she'd threatened to return."

"But why after all these years?" King Ailani asked. Cristos remained quiet, sipping his whiskey as he listened to the others.

Although Septima had expected Otera to respond, Bremusa spoke again.

"She is returning to prevent the prophecy of the Shadow Glass from coming to pass, the prophecy that got Otera's grandmother, mother, and sister murdered."

Seeing how her sister stiffened, Septima reached out and held Aurelia's hand. They'd both lost their mother to Joneira's henchmen, and not to a plague as they'd always been told. Aurelia leaned forward in her chair.

"What prophecy? Is it the same one that Variel told us?"

Bremusa leaned forward in her chair, the silver of her eyes like swirling melted silver.

"When I spoke to the Shadow Glass more than two decades ago, it predicted Messalina would have a daughter with a human mate, and that daughter would be chosen by the crown to serve over a combined northern kingdom. Messalina left her home as barely an adult, left her realm to find her human mate and do her part to fulfill the prophecy, to save her kingdom. She died to keep that future queen safe. Now Aurelia is of age, and Joneira aims to stop her from fulfilling the prophecy she tried to prevent years ago."

Chapter 29

Aurelia

Blood turned to ice in Aurelia's veins, and her breath caught in her throat, her chest tightening at Bremusa's words. Bremusa was the legendary elemental she'd only heard about before, the one who'd spoken the prophecy she'd learned about while at Variel's cottage months prior. She knew about the prophecy, and she knew her mother had been killed by one of Joneira's supporters after she'd stolen the Aegrician throne.

What Aurelia never knew was that her father had been part of that prophecy, or that she herself had been the entire basis for the prophecy that had sent her mother out of her kingdom in the first place. Holding her sister's hand tightly, her heart threatened to break in two. Her mother had died to protect her and her ascension to the throne, a throne in a world she had never even known existed.

"Why would the throne choose me to rule? I don't even have any magic."

There was so much more Aurelia needed to know, but she started there. She was nowhere near qualified to be a queen. She'd been pushing back against marrying Cristos to avoid being queen up until only recently.

Bremusa turned to her, the swirling of her eyes making it impossible for Aurelia to look away.

"You do have magic, Aurelia. Your ability to see through the eyes of others, to walk like a spirit in their lives, will only get stronger the longer you are in your ancestral land."

Remembering her conversation with Exie only days ago, Aurelia turned to look at her friend, who was sitting next to Septima. Exie nodded at her, the side of her mouth tipping up in a smile.

"Would you be able to show me how to use my abilities, Bremusa? Or do you know of someone else who could do so?"

With a genuine smile on her face, Bremusa nodded.

"Your mother was my best friend. I would be honored to help you learn to use your powers."

Cristos' hand slid to her thigh, squeezing gently to offer support as he turned to face the other monarchs.

"We need to talk about what's coming and how best to protect the city while we take Aegricia. Has there been any word about how far out the invaders are?"

King Ailani nodded, chewing a bite of the meat the servants had just placed on platters on the table.

"My flyers say the ships should be docking at any moment, so my guess would be that they will be upon Norithae within three days, four at the most."

"Then we should get rest tonight and march on Aegricia as soon as the weather clears," Cristos said to the room at large. "We need to try to retake the kingdom before the invaders arrive. If we have fewer enemies to fight at once, maybe we'll have a better shot at taking back Aegricia before we must face whatever is coming. We will need a way into the city, though. We need the wards taken down."

Finishing off the rest of her whiskey, Bremusa leaned forward in her chair, placing her hands flat against the table.

"I can take them down."

They spent a bit more time discussing the march into Aegricia and plans for Bremusa to take down the wards before retrieving the crown where it was hidden in the caves of the Shadow Glass, a magical mirror that gave her prophecies. If all else failed, Bremusa intended to destroy the crown, which would in turn destroy the portal, making it impossible for Warbotach, or anyone else, to cross into the human lands.

After plans were set in place for the days to come, Cristos and Aurelia left for their suite, as everyone else went to rest as well. There were still warriors and guards watching the perimeter of the palace grounds, however, and others reinforcing masking wards regularly to make the palace and surrounding lands invisible. Guards and warriors were set on a rotating duty schedule, allowing everyone time to get adequate rest when they were not needed for protection.

Watching the icy rain falling across the palace grounds from the balcony window, Aurelia sipped on a glass of water as Cristos stood behind her with his arms around her waist. The feel of his muscular body against hers always grounded her, made her feel so much safer.

"Hopefully the rain clears up soon, so it'll be safe to march north tomorrow."

There was a confidence in Cristos' words that Aurelia did not feel. They would march into battle again, and there was no guarantee any of them would walk out of it alive. Her stomach was in knots and her chest threatened to squeeze the breath from her lungs. She knew she couldn't survive in a world where Cristos or Septima didn't exist, and that terrified her.

There was more than just the war filling her with trepidation, however. Her monthly bleeding was late, and she was too afraid to tell him. If he knew she was potentially pregnant, he would insist she go to the camp with the rest of those who couldn't fight, and she wasn't willing to do that. If he and her sister were going to fight, then she needed to be there with them, even if only to work with the healers.

Sensing her emotions, he set their glasses down on a side table, pulling her around to face him and cupping her cheeks with his hands.

"Something is on your mind, and don't tell me it's just the war, because I can sense that it's not. What's wrong?"

His finger stroked her jaw, the gentle touch luring her eyes to close. She hesitated to respond for a moment, not ready to tell him the truth but knowing she couldn't keep it from him either. When she reopened her eyes, his face was only inches away as he leaned in and gave her a gentle kiss on the lips.

"You know you can tell me anything, my love. There is *nothing* you can't tell me."

Searching his face, she knew he meant every word. Blowing out a deep breath to calm her fears, she decided to tell him the truth.

"I don't know how to say this so I'm just going to say it plainly. My monthly bleeding is a few weeks late. I think I'm pregnant."

For a moment, Cristos did not respond. He only looked at her, each second of silence only tightening her chest more. Just when she'd nearly pulled away from him to walk away and busy herself, a smile spread across his face and he swooped her up into his arms.

"This is wonderful news, my love. The best news."

Setting her back down on her feet, he scanned her face again.

"Unless this isn't something you wanted..."

In better circumstances, circumstances in which she wouldn't have to worry about losing those closest to her, she would have probably been overjoyed, but she didn't want to tell Cristos that. She didn't want to ruin his happiness.

"I just wish it was better timing. I wish this baby would be coming when war wasn't looming over us like a dark cloud and I didn't have to worry about what our future held. When I bring a baby into the world, I want the world to be safe."

He kissed her again, slow and cherishing.

"This baby only gives us more to fight for. We need to make Ekotoria safe again, not just for our baby, but for all the children on this continent."

Cristos wrapped his arms around her, lifting her and carrying her to the bed before pulling her on top of him.

"You know."

She smirked, trailing her finger down his chest.

"This is the kind of thing that got us into this mess."

Lips spreading into a devilish grin, Cristos pulled her forward and nuzzled into her neck, his tongue and mouth kissing up her neck before finding their way back to her lips. "And I don't regret a thing."

Even with the war on her mind, and a pregnancy she knew she wasn't ready for, his skilled tongue teased her until her body craved more, making the thoughts of the next day flee her mind, at least for the moment. When he pulled away to catch his breath, she yanked him back to her, all her passion pouring into the kiss.

With her legs straddling him, his cock lined up perfectly with her sex, the press of it against the sensitive bud at her center sending shudders of pleasure through her. Her hips rolled against him, the cloth of his trousers between them maddening as his cock dragged along her cunt. Even with his trousers between them, the sensation was ecstasy, her back arching with the pleasure of it as she moaned against his mouth.

Sitting upright, Aurelia tugged off her tunic and tossed it to the floor, Cristos pulling her back to him and taking the peak of her breast into his mouth. He kissed and sucked as he lifted his hips to meet hers, the sensation against her most sensitive spot nearly bringing her to climax.

"I love you," he said as his mouth left her breast and he pulled her into another kiss, his tongue caressing hers in a sensual dance as he rubbed his shaft against her folds.

"If you love me, you'll help me take these off."

Desperate to feel his skin against hers, Aurelia fumbled with the buckle of her trousers, sliding to the side so she could remove them, Cristos using the moment to take his off as well.

She gazed at his body for a moment, at the rippling muscles beneath sun kissed skin, at the impressive cock that jutted in the air as he laid on the bed, watching her. Even his massive wings, that were just as black as his hair, turned her on.

When she climbed back on top of him, Cristos snaked his arm around her and flipped her onto her back before crawling on top of her. Sliding his hand between their bodies, he grasped his cock and traced her folds in teasing circles using the tip that already glistened with precum. She groaned, her hips bucking as she grinded against him.

Sensing her need, he slid his cock toward her entrance, dipping it in her wetness. Before she could complain about not wanting to wait anymore, Cristos thrust inside her, slamming all the way to the hilt. Pulling her legs over his shoulders, he lifted her hips with his hands, angling her body where he hit the most sensitive spot inside of her. Her moans turned to screams as he filled her completely, every stroke bringing her closer to fracturing.

"You feel so damn perfect, my mate."

Her body begged for release, her belly clenching tighter as he thrusted inside her. Sliding one hand from her hip to her folds, Cristos' thumb stroked her sensitive clit, his ministrations pulling her closer and closer toward climax. When her orgasm finally hit her with the intensity of a lightning storm, she bit into the pillow trying to quiet her screams. Cristos leaned forward and kissed her, the kiss absorbing her moans as his own release hit him a moment later. They collapsed against each other, satisfied and in love as Aurelia fell asleep with no thought of war in her mind.

Chapter 30

Aurelia

When Aurelia woke the next morning, it was not Cristos at her side, but her sister. Lying next to her on the bed, Septima stroked her hair, the touch reminding her of times before they'd left their home in Vaekros. Aurelia stretched, taking in Septima's beautiful features.

"I like your hair like this," she said, as she smoothed her sister's long braid over her shoulder. "Where is everybody?"

Flopping onto her back, Septima interlaced their fingers.

"The rain stopped sometime during the night, so Cristos and the military leaders are trying to get everything ready for those who will be marching toward Aegricia."

Although Aurelia had not intended to tell anyone else, she believed she was pregnant, she knew she had to tell her sister or face Septima's wrath when she did find out. Rolling over on her side, she loosened a breath, trying to steady her nerves.

Even if they had not been facing a war, becoming a mother was something she hadn't seen for herself at that point in her life.

"There's something I need to tell you, sissy."

The side of her mouth lifting into a smirk, Septima's face was full of mischief. "You're pregnant."

For a moment, Aurelia lost her ability to speak, but it passed quickly. "How did you know?"

Her sister's smirk spread into a toothy grin, and she threw her arms around her, squeezing Aurelia tight enough to force the air from her lungs.

"I knew something was different about you the moment I saw you in the foyer when I got back. You're not hiding it as well as you think you are, sissy."

"I'm not hiding it at all!"

Aurelia threw herself onto her back, staring at the ceiling as she wondered whether she was lying to Septima and to herself. Although she didn't know for sure, because she hadn't yet seen a healer, she'd wondered about this for at least a week before telling Cristos.

"I only told Cristos last night. I haven't even seen a healer to confirm."

Placing her hand on Aurelia's stomach, Septima let out a deep sigh.

"Well, you should see a healer right away, especially with the war coming in the next few days, but I have little doubt that you're with child. Actually, Exie called it before I did. She said she's been smelling it on you for weeks but had been too preoccupied with my capture to mention it."

Aurelia groaned, placing her hand on her sister's.

"Great! If Exie could smell it on me, then I wonder who else can as well."

Rolling off the side of the bed, Septima reached out her hands to help her sister up. "Well, come on. We should get you to the palace healer so she can check everything before you go trying to march into battle."

Dressing quickly in a tunic and trousers, Aurelia washed her face and cleaned her teeth before pulling on her boots and following her sister out of the bedchamber and toward the healer's rooms.

Although she'd never been to the palace infirmary, Aurelia knew exactly where it was after having been given directions by Cristos before they'd gone to bed. She hadn't said anything to Septima, but her mate had already insisted she see the healer in the morning to be examined. He didn't want her to take any chances if she was carrying their child.

He'd taken the news much better than she'd expected him to, and his joy at learning he would be a father had allowed her to sleep peacefully after they'd made love.

As she walked to the healer, however, Aurelia found herself thinking about her mother and everything she'd learned in the meeting the night before. She thought about how frightened her mother must've been to leave her realm all by herself, and how much pressure the prophecy had placed on her shoulders. She couldn't imagine being told that she had to find a mate in a different world to create a daughter who would save her kingdom someday.

The whole thing sounded so fanciful, and it would have been unbelievable if it were not for the fact that Aurelia knew the prophecy was true. Variel had said as much when they'd stayed at her cabin and she had learned the truth about her lineage. She'd learned she was not the human girl she always thought she was.

If only she could speak to her mother and tell her how brave she thought she was, and how much she loved her and appreciated what she'd done to bring her into the world. Messalina may have died when her children were small, but she'd been an amazing mother. She had given her children all of her, and had sacrificed herself to save them, to protect them from someone who would commit unspeakable acts to steal the throne from her family.

Joneira knew she could never fully be queen if the crown did not choose her, so she would have never been given the power over the portal, but it didn't seem like she cared about that. All she'd cared about was sitting on the throne and wielding power she didn't truly have, which was why they had been able to get rid of her and put Otera on the throne after less than a decade.

Aurelia didn't know every detail about what had happened back then. She knew Joneira had her mother murdered, but she hadn't known Joneira had killed her great grandmother, the female having been queen for nearly a century, nor that she'd killed her grandmother as well.

She wanted to talk to Otera and learn more about her mother and about how Otera had survived those years when Joneira had been in power. Her aunt must have gone through such devastation, losing her mother and grandmother, her sister, and her kingdom, all within a handful of years. Even though Aurelia had never known the elderly women, the knowledge of the tragedy of her family hurt her heart.

As they approached the entrance to the infirmary, Aurelia promised herself that, when she left, she would find her aunt and talk to her. There was so much she needed to know. She hoped that wherever she found Otera, she would find Bremusa as well, because the elemental had told her that her mother had been her best friend and had promised to help her with her magic. With the war coming at any moment, and Aurelia's powers still being new and untested, there was no time to waste before learning how to wield them, just in case she could be useful in the war.

Although most of the palace had painted walls, the corridor leading to the healer's rooms were stone, similar to the corridor in the dungeon. Since both spaces were on the lower levels of the palace, Aurelia assumed that was why.

When they walked into the room, the first thing she saw, aside from the many shelves and cabinets filled with bottles of potions and dried herbs, was an elderly Norithaean female leaning over a counter with her large black wings tucked in against her back. When the healer turned around to face them, still wiping her hands on a rag, her eyes went wide.

"I've been wondering when you were going to come to me, milady."

Taking a few steps toward Aurelia, the female's head tipped to the side.

"You are with child, are you not?"

Aurelia nodded as she entered the room with Septima by her side.

"And you could tell that by just looking at me?'

The fae truly were more skilled at detecting things about a person, which made Aurelia wonder what else they could tell about a person just by smelling them. Suddenly she felt quite uncomfortable.

The healer chuckled and moved around the space, waving Aurelia over and indicating for her to sit on top of an examination table. With only a moment of hesitation, she did as she was asked.

"We fae can tell a lot about a person by their scent. Before you were with child, your scent was that of a half-human, half-Aegrician female. Once you became pregnant with your mate, our king's child, a new scent mixed with yours, the scent of a Norithaean. Now that the king's scent has become part of yours, it will be hard to hide your pregnancy from others."

Although Aurelia did not think the healer was trying to scare her, her words did fill her with fear, fear for her child, fear for herself, and most of all, fear for her mate. If their enemies could detect that she was carrying the Norithaean king's child, they could use her as leverage against him. If she was taken hostage, with or without his child in her belly, Cristos would do anything to get her back, and their enemies would know that.

She could not march into battle, not if it put her child's life at risk, and not if it put Cristos' life at risk. Just thinking about him marching to Aegricia without her made the backs of her eyes burn and her stomach twist into knots. If something happened to him, she wanted to be there, she wanted to protect him, but with a life growing inside her, she couldn't, because the baby needed her protection more.

"Lie back right here so I can check the baby."

So lost in her own head, the healer's words took Aurelia by surprise. With Septima's help, she laid back on the table, Septima tucking a pillow behind her head as the healer moved in close to her and covered her with a sheet.

"I'm gonna need to check everything to make sure everything is in good working order. Would that be okay, milady?"

Aurelia nodded although she didn't know what kind of medical equipment was used for pregnancy in the fae realm, which made her admittedly nervous. She'd never been around anyone pregnant while living in the war camp in the forest.

"Can you help me remove your trousers, so I can check your belly?"

Aurelia nodded and reached to her buckle, but her sister moved in to help, unbuttoning her trousers and sliding them off her feet before returning to her side.

"Are the fae able to find out the sex of the baby before it's born?"

Septima asked, taking over the conversation because she knew her sister was distressed.

The healer nodded but lifted her arm in a slight shrug.

"We are sometimes able to tell the scent of the baby when it is big enough, but not always. We say that the strongest babies put off the strongest scent."

She chuckled, but the sound was warm.

"I would think our king Cristos would make a strong child, and that we will know sooner than later if it is a son or a daughter."

Aurelia remained still as the healer touched her belly, placing a glass against it to listen to the heartbeat. She wished she would be able to hear it herself, because that would make it more real to her. With her belly still flat, and no other signs of pregnancy showing, she didn't see a pregnant woman when she looked in the looking glass, but she knew that would change as her belly grew and the baby started to move inside her.

"From what I can tell, milady, the baby is strong and healthy. You are doing a wonderful job taking care of it in your belly. I will want you to check back with me at least once every two weeks, more if you have any trouble. Don't ever feel like you're being silly if you have a worry. I know as a first-time mother, it can be scary, so don't hesitate to come to me if you're worried about something, even if you're worried it's nothing."

Aurelia nodded, pulling herself up on her elbows as the healer walked away to allow Septima to help her back into her trousers.

It wasn't necessarily sad tears when a flutter of emotion hit Aurelia and she started to cry. She was overwhelmed but she knew they were happy tears. She and Cristos would have a baby together and they would be a family. They would create the world they said they would, and that was something to look forward to.

Chapter 31

Aurelia

Once they left the healer's rooms, Septima and Aurelia headed toward the barracks where they expected to find Cristos, Exie, and the rest of the military, who were planning the attack on Warbotach. She wanted to talk to Cristos, but she also wanted to speak to Otera. She hoped to be able to talk to both of them before the armies left, because then it would be too late.

The air outside was still frigid from the icy rain the night before. Aurelia pulled her cloak closer to her body to protect her from the wind as a shadow flew overhead. She lifted her eyes to the sky to see one of the dragons from Diapolis flying over the palace before turning toward the sea. Seeing them always took her breath away. They were such majestic yet terrifying creatures.

Entering the barracks, there was a flurry of activity as soldiers from all three kingdoms moved around the space, going in and out of different rooms and talking amongst themselves. She could hear the clatter of swords as warriors trained in the rooms suited for that. Usually, when the weather was nice, they would train out on the grounds, but with the icy rain that had left the grounds wet and the air still too cold, it appeared many of the warriors chose the more comfortable option to train before they were forced out into the elements to either march or fly to the northern kingdom.

In the barracks meeting room, she found Cristos and Otera, along with Blaedia, King Ailani, and several other military leaders. Taryn and Lars had also returned from the civilian camp in the valley and were sitting side-by-side against the wall, with mugs of hot tea in their hands. As soon as Cristos saw her, a bright smile crossed his lips, and he crossed the room to her, pulling her into his arms and kissing her deeply.

"Good morning, beautiful."

Lifting her off the ground, he kissed her again.

"I take it you went to the healer this morning?"

She nodded, not yet ready to talk about it in front of everyone else. When he pulled away, the giant smile still graced his face and his blue eyes were the brightest she'd ever seen them.

"We'll be finished up here soon and then you and I can get some lunch and talk about what she said."

With one more kiss, Cristos set her down on the ground and turned back toward King Ailani, continuing a conversation she must have interrupted when she'd walked in.

Catching Queen Otera's eye, Aurelia approached her and asked if they could talk privately. Nodding, her aunt followed her out of the room and into another that was usually used for training but was currently vacant. Blaedia had watched them leave the room, but merely touched her lover on the hand and remained behind.

When they were in the private space and the door was closed, Otera pulled her niece into her arms, squeezing her tight and caressing her back with her hand. Guiding Aurelia to one of the benches along the wall, Otera and her niece sat down, still arm-in-arm.

"I was hoping you would find me this morning," Otera said, her face a picture of joy. "You look so much like your mother."

Aurelia studied her aunt's face for a moment before responding.

"So, do you."

Although Otera smiled, Aurelia could see the pain behind her eyes.

"My mother is why I wanted to speak to you. So much was said last night that I didn't know, and I need to know more. I hoped you could tell me more about my mother and about what she went through to have me."

Otera nodded, taking Aurelia by the hand.

"Let me first say that your mother, Messalina, never wanted to be queen. Although we do not have power over who the crown chooses, Messalina always hoped it would not choose her. When Bremusa consulted the Shadow Glass, as our grandmother's time on the throne was coming to an end, the Shadow Glass told Bremusa, who is a powerful oracle, that Messalina's daughter would be queen, and that the child would come from a union between her and a human mate. The Shadow Glass predicted that Messalina's daughter would combine the kingdoms of the north as queen and would bring peace to the continent at last."

"On the night Joneira and her henchman raided the palace and killed my grandmother, Messalina and I were not at the party. We'd left not long before to go find Bremusa, who had gone that morning into the caves to consult the Shadow Glass again and had not returned. We were concerned something had happened to her and so we took Blaedia and a few other fighters and had them carry us to the caves so we could look for her."

Going silent for a moment, Otera blew out a breath.

"By the time we got to the caves, it was clear something was wrong. Bremusa had been held in place by chains made of dragon bone. They were enchanted to harm her if she tried to escape, and it took powerful magic to get her free. We discovered that Joneira and her supporters had gone to the caves when Bremusa was there and had tortured her to get her to reveal the secrets of the Shadow Glass. Joneira wanted to know if she would be able to take power. She wanted to know how to take it by force. After Bremusa gave her little information, she was chained and left in the caves. A ward over the cave entrance prevented anyone from entering, and her from exiting, so just to get into the cave itself took time. The Shadow Glass told Joneira that in order to take the throne, she would have to kill the queen and the queen's descendants, because although the crown is not passed on in families, the crown intended to pass to the queen's granddaughter...*Me*. Messalina never went back to the palace after that night. With Joneira knowing about the prophecy and knowing it would be Messalina's child who took the throne and combined the kingdoms, it was not safe for her to return to the palace. We knew that Joneira was already on her way back to the palace to kill our grandmother. With a bag Bremusa had packed weeks before and hidden in the cave, Messalina was sent through the portal on the back of one of the warriors and forced to go to the human realm to look for her mate. I was sent into hiding while the warriors went back to the palace to try to stop the inevitable."

When Aurelia turned to look at her aunt, Otera's cheeks were damp from her tears.

"I never saw my sister again after that night. I never spoke to my sister again after she left the caves on the back of that phoenix. We exchanged ravens for years, but the ravens stopped when she lost her life."

A sob broke from Otera with that last admission and Aurelia wrapped her arms around her aunt, her own tears sliding down her cheeks.

"We'd always intended, when she'd left that night, that she would return when it was safe, but she died before that ever happened. We knew about you and your brother, but it was safest for you to remain with your father. Drawing any attention to you with Joneira still alive would have put your life at risk so we didn't take any chances."

Aurelia sniffed and wiped the moisture from her cheek.

"Did my father know what my mother was?"

Otera nodded, giving Aurelia's hand a gentle squeeze.

"From the messages we received from your mother, your father knew everything. They were very much in love. If there was any good in my sister having to leave, it's that she knew love, true love, and she had you and your brother. Those things make her life worthwhile."

The emotions that warred inside Aurelia made her chest ache. Pain and confusion, love and hope, all battled inside her. Turning to face her aunt, Aurelia tucked the hair behind her ear.

"There's something I need to tell you, Aunt Otera."

She hesitated, debating if she wanted to tell anyone else her secret.

"I'm pregnant."

The grin returning to Otera's face, she pulled Aurelia into a hug, kissing her on the cheek.

"That's wonderful news, Aurelia. Your mother would be so proud of you. This gives us so much more to fight for, and when we win against Warbotach, we will win for your baby, the heir to the combined kingdoms of northern Ekotoria, because I will be stepping down when you become queen of Norithae. The prophecy must come to pass."

Chapter 32

Kason

Packing their belongings for the journey north, Kason and Holera prepared to leave Norithae with a group of warriors that would head closer to Aegricia and begin the process of trying to remove the wards around the city. They intended to set up camp in the caves nearby and use the combined powers of those who had warding abilities to begin chipping away at those protections put in place by Warbotach. Bremusa, being a powerful elemental, would be joining them on their journey because she claimed to be able to take down the wards on her own.

Leaving just before sunset, Kason slung their bags over his shoulder and holstered his sword and bow, following Holera into the palace courtyard, where the other warriors were already ready to go. She shifted in a flash of fire and Kason climbed onto her back, settling himself in as he always did.

In a flap of her beautiful silver wings, she launched them into the sky aiming toward the mountains that separated Norithae from Aegricia.

The night air was cold, the storms from the night before having left the air still feeling like winter when spring should have been setting in. Kason pulled his cloak tighter around his body, fastening the fur hood over his head and pulling a scarf in front of his face. The cold wind didn't seem to bother his mate when in her phoenix form, but the higher they went into the clouds, the more uncomfortable it was for him.

Not wanting Warbotach to know their intentions, the group of Phoenix and Norithae fighters flew high over the mountains, only swooping down low once they had bypassed the city all together and could land safely near the caves without being seen.

Landing in a small valley between the mountain peaks, Kason was glad the mountains blocked the wind. Finding firewood to keep them warm would be difficult, however, since the area that far into the mountains did not have many trees. Thankfully, most of the group had packed some just in case.

The other warriors landing nearby, the Phoenixes shifted back into their fae forms with a flare of fire, and the group set out in search of a comfortable cave where they could spend their time without being seen by their enemies.

Already knowing the area because of her time having to go to the caves where the Shadow Glass was, the place where she received many of her prophecies, Bremusa showed them to a location where they could be safe and warm while trying to work on the wards.

Setting up camp several hours before sunrise, Kason and Holera escorted the elemental to the boundary of the wards around the city, standing guard as she assessed the protections the Warbotach mages had put into place.

Kason held his hand on the hilt of his sword, keeping his senses alert as he scanned the darkness around them. Although the Warbotach leaders would not have expected them to set up camp in the mountains behind the city, it did not mean they didn't have patrols in that area.

Bremusa walked the perimeter of the area, not in the form of a female, but in the form of a large black wolf. A predator hunting for its prey was all the barbarian fighters would have seen if they'd come across her. Being an elemental, Bremusa could shift into nearly any creature, giving herself the ability to mask who she was altogether so her power would not be used against the Aegrician people.

Holera patrolled near Kason's side. Although she was a warrior and could protect herself, he didn't want his mate too far away from him where he could not protect her if someone did show up to attack. There were more dangers in those mountains than just their enemies. Many vicious creatures hunted through the mountains and caves, as well as the forest land beyond, creatures they didn't yet know existed but could tear her to shreds before she had the chance to shift and fly away. As long as he was alive, he would always protect her just as he loved her, with his last breath.

Camouflaged in the darkness of the night, the elemental female had moved out of sight shortly after they began their watch in the area. All had been silent for at least an hour or two, until the sound of pounding footsteps approached Kason and Holera from the darkness.

Reaching for his mate, he pulled Holera against his chest, backing up toward the caves and holding his sword aloft to strike whatever was coming to attack. His heart pounded wildly, expecting a hellhound or another bloodthirsty beast to burst out of the darkness when it was too late for him to see it and strike. Relief washed over him when it wasn't a bloodthirsty beast that approached them from the shadows, but Bremusa in her wolf form, running straight toward them and into the caves behind them.

It only took a moment for him to see what she was running from- a mountain wendigo. Before he could think, Kason lifted Holera, tossing her over his shoulder and bolting toward the cave. Wendigos were flesh-eating monsters, vicious creatures who had strength, speed, and sharp claws. They did not need weapons as he did.

The creature gained on him, swiping just out of its reach as he ran, the creature's claws grazing the side of his arm. He hissed, but didn't stop, running faster than he had in a long time to get his mate to safety.

A blast of icy air hit him from the front as Bremusa stood in the opening of the cave, arms in the air, shooting power like he had never seen toward the creature.

"Get behind me! NOW!" She screamed over the sound of the wind erupting from her fingertips.

It was not easy to rush through the bursts of icy wind that swirled like a tornado around him but he clenched his jaw and held Holera tightly against his chest and forged ahead, making it into the cave just as the animal screamed, swept up and unable to fight the cyclone of wind coming from the elemental.

Once inside the cave, Kason set his mate down on the ground and she immediately reached towards his arm to assess his wound.

"Kason, come in the tent with me so I can dress this wound right away. You're bleeding pretty heavily."

He wanted to go back to the cave's entrance and help the others fight the beast in case it got past Bremusa's powers, but before he had a chance to argue, his mate pulled him by his non-injured arm. She would not have taken no for an answer. So, instead of twisting out of her grip, he followed her into their tent to let her take care of him.

By the time Kason and Holera made it back out of the tent, his arm cleaned with a fresh bandage, the activity at the cave's entrance had mostly died down. A few fighters guarded just inside the cave, but the beast was gone.

Bremusa sat near the fire in her fae form, leaning over one of the Norithae warriors who had joined them, the male bleeding heavily from a gash in his leg. They darted forward to see if they could help, although neither of them was a healer.

"What happened? What can we do?" Holera asked as she kneeled next to Bremusa, reaching to put pressure on the wound.

Moving away as Holera covered the wound, Bremusa dug through her satchel.

"A few of the warriors ran forward to try to kill the beast while I used magic to hold it in place, but it lashed out and got his leg before the other warrior sliced its head off. All we can do now is try to stop the bleeding."

Lowering himself to his knees, Kason leaned forward to help his mate, pressing his hands against the male's leg as the Norithaean laid unconscious.

"How will you work on the wards if there are wendigos in this area? If there's one, then there are more."

Approaching the injured male again, Bremusa leaned over him, Holera moving her hands away as the other female applied a balm to the wound, the substance slowing the flow of blood to merely a trickle. Seeming to be happy with the progress, she reached for a roll of bandages and wrapped them around the male's leg, covering the wound.

"I'm going to go back out tomorrow, but I will go in my true form and no one is to follow me."

Chapter 33

Aurelia

By the time Aurelia finished talking to Otera and they'd left the training room to return to the others, the military leaders and monarchs were already filing out of the meeting room, everyone dispersing in different directions. Catching her eye, Cristos smiled and walked toward her, wrapping his arm around her waist and kissing her on the forehead.

"Are you hungry, my love? We could probably go to the kitchen and see what they're cooking, or if you'd like, we can take food back to our rooms."

The way he always tried to take care of her made Aurelia grin against his chest as she walked nestled below his shoulder.

"Do you know if Septima will be going into the kitchen?"

Although she and Christos needed to talk, she would've liked to sit down and eat with her sister if possible, especially since they would be leaving for war within a day.

"I believe Septima and Exie have flown out over the forest so Septima can practice her archery."

Although she really wanted to spend more time with her sister, Aurelia understood Septima's need to train. With them going into battle, she realized training may have been more important at that moment than lunch. Still, she promised herself that she would at least try to have dinner with Septima that night, maybe even eat with everyone. It may have been the last opportunity they would be able to spend together, which was a painful thought. Even now, with Kason and Holera having already left for the Aegrician mountains along with Bremusa and a few other warriors, it was already too late for everyone to dine together.

"Since they're not available, let's get food brought to our rooms so we can talk in private and then maybe we will be able to have dinner with everyone tonight."

Christos nodded, his chin against the side of her head.

"I think everyone would like that very much."

Continuing through the palace, arm-in-arm, Cristos asked a servant to bring their meal to the suite and they headed up the stairs.

Turning to face her as soon as the door to their suite closed, Cristos pulled Aurelia into his arms, lifting her up and kissing her, his lips lingering for a moment. When he pulled away, she could see by the look on his face that he was more interested in talking about what she'd learned at the healer than what plans he'd made in the war room.

"What did the healer say to you about the baby? Is everything going to be okay? Are you and the baby healthy?"

Aurelia giggled at how rapidly the questions came out of him. He was indeed excited to be a father, and it warmed her heart to see him with so much hope and joy. Taking him by the hand, she led him to the sitting area in front of the fireplace, lowering herself onto the sofa as Cristos added a few logs to the stack, lighting a fire quickly.

"I wanted to talk to you about something else as well, my love," he said.

Approaching the sofa, Cristos sat next to her, taking her hands in his.

"The warriors are leaving tomorrow to go north, but before I go, I wanted to know if you would marry me. I love you more than life. If something happens to me, I need to know you and our child will be taken care of."

"Cristos... I..."

She hesitated, shaking her head slowly as she squeezed his hands tighter.

"You know I'll marry you, but please don't talk like that. Nothing is going to happen to you and you're not leaving without me. I've been thinking about it a lot, and I know I can't fight in the war with our baby inside me, but I'm still going with you. I can work in the healer's tents. I can help in some way, but I'm not staying behind. I just can't."

Warm tears slid down her cheeks and Cristos swiped them away with his thumb.

"I don't want you or our baby anywhere near Warbotach. I don't know what I would do if something happened to you—to either of you."

Dropping his hand from her face, he placed it on her belly that was still flat, no sign of her pregnancy showing yet.

"I know I just found out he or she is growing inside you, but it's all I've been able to think about. This child is a promise of a better future for our kingdom. It's something good when there's so much bad, a new life when there will be so much death. After what happened to Septima at the battle when we took back my kingdom, I can't take a chance of the same thing happening to you. While you're here, you're safe. The palace is warded, so even if the invaders to the continent passed through Norithae to get to Aegricia, they wouldn't be able to get into the palace grounds. They won't be able to get to you. I can't protect you like that if you come with me."

"I understand your point, but it doesn't change my mind. There's no way you and my sister are leaving this kingdom without me, pregnant or not."

His face tensing, Cristos remained quiet for an agonizing moment, the moment only interrupted by a knock on the door. Rising before she could, he crossed the room and answered the door, taking their meal from the servant and setting it on the table. She followed him to the table and sat down, her stomach already growling.

"And you will stay with the healers?" Cristos asked, his eyes searching her face. "If you come north with us, you'll remain in the warded camps?"

Knowing she couldn't promise what he was asking, it took Aurelia a heartbeat to nod. She intended to stay in the camps and help the healers, but she knew she would leave the camp in an instant if she received word that he or her sister was injured.

"I will stay in the camps, but I have conditions."

When he turned up to look at her as he placed their food into plates, there was a curious look on his face, one eyebrow arched in that way she loved.

"Conditions?"

Taking a bite of the delicious casserole the servant had brought to them, she had to chew her food before she could answer.

"Yes. I don't know if it's possible, but I want to find Variel and take her with us. She's a powerful healer. That's what you told me when we met, when she healed Exie from both physical and magical wounds. Between her being a healer and an oracle, and her ability to shift, she would be really helpful in this war. We need her."

The look on Cristos' face was contemplative as he took a sip of his whiskey.

"She may be difficult to find, but we can certainly try. Although…"

He hesitated, his eyes going distant before he turned them back to her.

"Variel left this palace when my mother was murdered and has chosen to live away from society ever since. We may find her only to discover she doesn't want to join us in this war at all."

"I do understand that, but we have to at least try. We have to go to her and give her that option. Plus, she seemed to know so much about what changes I would go through when I came into my fae body, and into my powers. I feel like I need to learn more from her. Maybe I can find a way to help in this war if I can learn more about my powers."

"If I say yes, that we will look for Variel tomorrow, then will you marry me tonight?"

Nearly choking on her food at the urgency of his question, Aurelia took a sip of her tea.

"You really want to get married tonight?"

Cristos smiled, his blue eyes bright.

"The armies are leaving tomorrow. Septima, Exie, and Otera intend to join them, as do I. It may not be the wedding you'd hoped for, at least not until the war is over, but Septima and your aunt will be there if we do it tonight, as will some of our friends. When the armies march north tomorrow, you and I will go south to Variel. With or without her, we can find our way back to the armies before nightfall tomorrow night. I know where they plan to camp."

The rest of the afternoon went by quickly once they'd decided. Cristos left their suite to plan for the event while Aurelia spent time with her sister, needing to do some planning of her own.

With the little time they had, and everything else that needed to be done, there was no time to look for a dress or plan the kind of party she would've had in Vaekros, but as Cristos said, they would plan a grander wedding ceremony once they returned from war, once they *won* the war. Along with the baby growing inside her, the wedding would be one more thing to look forward to.

By the time Aurelia found her sister in the kitchens, she and Exie having only recently returned from training in the forest, it was clear the entire palace knew there would be a wedding that night. The underlying mood was tense, but the wedding lifted spirits, if only a little.

"A lot of changes going on in your life right now, sissy."

Taking a seat next to Septima and Exie, her sister's brilliant grin was infectious.

"You're growing up all of a sudden."

Aurelia snorted, reaching for the fresh bread on the table in front of her.

"I may be doing grown up things, but I don't feel like I'm ready for any of it."

Kissing Exie on the cheek, Septima stood from the table.

"Let's go find something for you to wear."

"Where? We can't leave the palace grounds to go into town, not now. I doubt anything is even open."

Her grin only spreading wider, Septima reached down her hand for Aurelia's.

"We may not be able to go into town, but one of the servants let slip that Cristos' mother's gowns are still in the palace. His father never parted with them. I was asked to bring you to find her when you came down, so we can choose a dress for you to wear tonight."

Chapter 34

Aurelia

The rooms where Cristos' father had resided were opulent, but it was clear one of the barbarians had used the space for his own needs when they'd taken the city. There were damages to some of the furniture and slashes in a few of the walls from a blade, but the servants had done their best to fix up what they could.

Aurelia and Septima followed the elderly servant, a female named Maelia, through the gilded space and into a large dressing room, the walls lined with wooden floor to ceiling cabinets.

"King Marcellus was a loving husband to Queen Cordia. Her death nearly broke him, as it did her son."

Heart breaking for her mate, Aurelia watched as Maelia opened one of the cabinets, the space filled with the most beautiful gowns she'd ever seen.

"He never gave his heart to another female and kept all her things safely tucked away. If the king was here today, he would be filled with joy for his son, but since he's not," she said, holding her hand up in an invitation for Aurelia to look at the dresses, "I know he would be happy that his beloved's dresses are being given to his son's new wife."

With a sweet smile on her face, Maelia stepped aside to allow Aurelia access to the opened cabinet. Not knowing what to look at first, her hand moved across the dresses, allowing the exquisite fabrics to slide through her fingers. Although she didn't recognize some of the fabrics, many felt like satin and others were dripping with lace or trimmed with jewels. She didn't know how she would've been able to choose one of them when they were all so beautiful, but her sister didn't seem to share the same difficulty.

"This one."

Slipping past her, Septima dug her hands into the closet, pulling out a gold embroidered ivory dress with long skirts that flared away from a fitted waist. Holding it in front of herself in the looking glass, Aurelia admired the intricate designs expertly sewn across the bodice.

"I think it might already be your size, sissy."

As she held the dress against her body, she agreed.

"Should I try it on?"

If she were being honest, she was a little uncomfortable wearing Cristos' mother's clothing, not because his mother had worn it before, but because she didn't want to ruin it. Also, she didn't know how Cristos would respond to seeing her in something his father had held onto for so long because it was important to him and their family. The servant, however, truly believed it would be acceptable for her to wear the queen's clothing, and she trusted her judgment, only hoping it didn't upset anybody to have the queen's clothes be given away.

Taking the dress from her hand, Septima worked to remove it from the hanger as Aurelia and the servant untied her tunic and trousers, her clothing dropping to the floor. When she was left in only her underclothes, Septima helped her to pull the dress on, going behind her to lace up the back.

Although she'd spent most of her life in the human lands in dresses and gowns, she'd only worn one since entering Ekotoria. The emerald dress she'd worn in Diapolis to attend King Ailani's party had been beautiful, breathtaking even, but it had been nothing compared to the ivory and gold dress that had once belonged to the queen of Norithae.

"This is the one," Septima said, and Aurelia couldn't have agreed more. In that dress, with her crimson hair and bright blue eyes, she knew she looked stunning.

"Yes, this is the one."

After leaving the royal chambers with her dress, Septima, Aurelia, and the servant went back to her and Cristos' quarters so they could help her get ready. As Maelia started her bath, Septima went to her own quarters to find Exie and Cristos. She also intended to find out more about the ceremony, what time it would take place and where it would be located. She also, Aurelia knew, was going to forbid Cristos from going back to their suite and seeing her before the wedding. Although her sister had not said so much, Aurelia knew she would be giving Cristos those orders.

By the time Aurelia got out of the bath, Septima was back and wearing a mischievous grin, Exie at her side. Drying off

"I just need to get my clothes, Exie," Cristos said with more amusement than agitation in his tone. Septima darted toward the door a moment later, responding "no" loudly enough for Aurelia to hear. She snickered but didn't get up from where she was sitting.

"You are not coming in this room and seeing my sister before the wedding and giving your marriage bad luck, Cristos. Just tell me what you want, and I will go get it for you."

Cristos groaned but agreed, explaining to Septima where to find the uniform he wanted to wear for the wedding. Only a moment later, her sister walked past her, going into the large wardrobe and pulling out a few pieces of clothing to give to Cristos at the door. They exchanged goodbyes, Cristos explaining where they would need to meet him and at what time, before he walked away, closing the door behind him.

Staring at herself one final time in the looking glass, Aurelia was taken aback by how stunning the gown was on her. What she would be getting married in was a dress that was made for a queen. It only took her a moment before the realization hit her that she was about to become a queen, something she never saw for herself.

The irony hit her a moment later at the words Otera had spoken to her only that morning. Her mother had never wanted to be queen either, but it was her daughter who'd been destined to be queen. It was almost as though the prophecy was coming to pass even before the war. By the end of the night she would be queen of Norithae, and when Otero stepped down after the war and allowed the crown to pick the prophesied queen, Aurelia would become queen of both kingdoms.

Just the thought of it squeezed at her chest, threatening to take the breath from her lungs. Life was moving too fast, the drastic changes too much for one person in such a short span of time. She knew she would adapt and overcome everything in her life that was happening, but it was still overwhelming at that moment. Taking in a deep breath, Aurelia exhaled slowly before sliding on the golden shoes that had also belonged to Cristos' mother and walked toward the door.

Following Septima, who had also changed into a beautiful gown, and Exie, who wore an immaculate soldier's uniform,

Aurelia left her suite and headed through the palace to the place where she would become Cristos' wife.

Entering the main ballroom, she was blown away by the beauty of the space. Candelabras and sconces lit the room, highlighting the beautiful artwork and sculptures that lined the walls. The glass doors in the back of the room were opened to a large balcony and the pastel sky beyond, as the sun set over the water. Light music fluttered down on the breeze, although Aurelia was unsure of what type of instrument was being played. Septima and Exie led her toward the balcony, stopping just outside as a servant scurried through the doorway to tell whoever was inside that she was ready. Only a moment later, the servant returned and ushered them inside.

Holding her sister's hand, just as she had when they'd entered the Aegrician war camp all those months ago when they'd left their home, Aurelia walked through the threshold and onto the balcony, her heart pounding wildly as she glanced around at her friends, and even those she'd never become acquainted with, all seated and waiting to witness the union.

Turning toward the sound of the music and seeing her mate standing in front of the balcony railing with the sunset at his winged back took Aurelia's breath away. He truly was the most gorgeous male, a perfect mate, and she couldn't believe he was hers and she was his.

The moment their eyes met, Cristos smiled, his eyes sparkling with joy at the sight of her. Smoothing out the front of his crisp, black tunic, he walked forward to take her hand.

"I believe I've seen that gown before," he said, as he pulled her to him and kissed her deeply. For a moment, the world around them disappeared as his lips caressed hers. "But I didn't realize it was still here. It looks beautiful on you. I'm so glad the servants kept my mother's clothing safe all this time and thought about showing this to you."

Some of the tension that had been building in her chest loosened at his words, relief flooding through her that he wasn't upset about her wearing his mother's dress.

"I have to admit, I wasn't sure if you would be unhappy with me for wearing something of your mother's."

Pulling away to scan her face, Cristos slid his hand down her cheek, the feeling sending shivers through her body, even with everyone watching.

"I would never be upset with you, and certainly not for that. I can't wait another moment to marry you, Aurelia. I know it's not the way that we wanted it to be, but once the war is over, we will have so much to celebrate, and another wedding will be just the way to do it. We'll have a big party with all our friends. We'll dine and dance, and then we will enjoy lots of time together before the baby comes."

The plans for their future sent the warmth of hope spreading through her chest. Kissing him again, she leaned her cheek against his chest, glancing back toward the railing where he had been standing. Her mouth dropped when she noticed the familiar face who stood there waiting for them. *Variel.*

Chapter 35

Aurelia

"You found her," Aurelia said, her tone incredulous. "How?"

"I didn't want us to not be able to leave with the army in the morning, so I went to look for her on my own while you spent time with Septima today."

Mouth opening and closing, she was speechless for a moment.

"Why didn't you tell me?"

Cristos smiled and kissed her on the head before wrapping his arm around her waist and leading her toward the shifter.

"I didn't want to worry you and I believed I would be able to find her quickly. Plus, I knew you would want to spend our final day here with your sister and I didn't want to take that away from you."

As soon as she approached Variel, Aurelia darted forward, wrapping the older female in her arms. It had only been a few months since she'd seen her, but in that moment, the shifter felt like family and family was what she needed. When Variel pulled away, a wide grin spread across her face.

"I told Cristos I wouldn't be leaving the forest to come into the city again, but he insisted I needed to come and marry you two, and *that* was an event I couldn't miss. Since I'm already here, I guess I might as well help in the war. It'll take all of us to win our kingdom back."

The backs of Aurelia's eyes burned with Variel's words. They meant more to her than Variel probably knew. Ever since she'd realized she was likely coming into her fae powers, she knew she needed to meet with Variel. She knew the woman who had been like a mother to Cristos ever since his own mother had been murdered would be able to teach her to use her powers for something good.

"I can't thank you enough for leaving your home to come here, Variel," Aurelia said, meaning the words so much more than she could even express. "I know it wasn't easy for you to leave your home, and I know you didn't intend to come to the city again, but it means so much to all of us that you're here."

The shifter nodded, patting Aurelia on the arm.

"I know there's a lot that we need to talk about, and we will. But let's get the two of you married first, and then you and I will talk later."

Aurelia glanced at Cristos before turning her eyes back to Variel.

"Wait a minute, you are going to marry us?"

She really didn't know anything about how marriages were conducted in the fae world, or who was responsible for conducting the ceremonies, but she had no idea Variel was able to do it. The healer nodded, a grin on her face.

"I am."

Otera and Septima walked up behind them, taking a place near Aurelia's side as Cristos reached out and held her hands. The moment felt surreal as Aurelia watched Variel murmur words to herself, and a momentary sense of panic hit her when the healer pulled a dagger from a sheath at her side, continuing to speak just under her breath.

"Give me your hands."

Although Cristos gave his hand right away, setting it facing up in Variel's right hand, Aurelia was hesitant after seeing the dagger, but blew out breath and turned her hand over, sliding it on top of Variel's left hand.

"In our world, unlike in the human world, it is the mating bond that determines when a male and a female have chosen each other to be their partner in life. Marriage is a second choosing, a way for you to tell the world that you belong to each other."

Placing Aurelia's hand on top of Cristos', Variel lifted the dagger and sliced it across Aurelia's palm, a hiss bursting through her teeth. She'd nearly pulled her hand away, but the intensity in Cristos' eyes told her not to, told her it would be okay, and for her to trust him.

Blood slid from the wound, pooling in her hand as Variel made an exact slice on Cristos' palm as well. A moment later their hands were joined, their blood mixing together as Variel wrapped their hands in a strip of cloth.

"As bonded mates, your bodies already knew your hearts beat for each other, but now your blood flows together, making you one. Wherever you go from here, and no matter what happens from here, you will always be connected. Your blood will always flow in each other's veins."

Placing her hands on either side of theirs, Variel murmured a few more words before warmth radiated from her hands, soothing the pain from the wounds she'd inflicted.

When Variel moved away, Cristos leaned forward, his lips finding Aurelia's, the kiss filled with enough emotion to bring tears to Aurelia's eyes. As soon as they pulled apart, cheers erupted from their family and friends, sending Aurelia back into Cristos' arms as she broke into a fit of giggles, the stress leading up to that moment dissolving away into joy. She knew it would fade by the next day when they marched toward war. For that moment, however, she had just married the love of her life, and for that night she wasn't going to let the thought of war ruin her joy.

After the wedding ceremony concluded, they'd spent the next few hours eating, drinking, and spending time with their friends as a few warriors played upbeat music. Aurelia had gotten to speak to Variel briefly, but with all the revelry, it had been too distracting to have such an important discussion. With the trip in front of them the next day, they agreed to talk then, or at least when they made camp on their way.

Aurelia and Cristos made it back up to their suite as everyone else turned in for the night. Although they would have liked to enjoy the festivities longer, the long journey ahead made it a smarter decision to go to bed early while they still had a soft bed to sleep in.

When they got back to their suite, Aurelia was completely exhausted, but she stifled back a yawn as her husband led her to the bathing room and turned on the tap over the tub. They took a bath quickly, both of them realizing how badly they needed sleep.

Once out of the bath, they crawled into bed, Aurelia already mourning the comfort of a real mattress and linens and dreading the nights she would be sleeping in a tent again. It was the least of all her worries however, since war brought many unthinkable outcomes, but she chose to put those as far from her mind as she could until she couldn't anymore. Sliding up against her husband's side, she breathed deeply, his sandalwood and spice scent always managing to calm her.

"How's your hand?" Cristos asked, flipping over her palm to check the wound that was barely visible. He grinned, kissing her palm. "It seems Variel is a good healer, indeed."

Aurelia yawned, her hand covering her mouth.

"She is, although I wish someone had warned me. That hurt."

Chuckling, Cristos rolled onto his side and pulled her against his chest.

"I'm sorry about that, but it feels better now?"

She nodded, rolling him onto his back and leaning over to kiss his chest.

"It does."

Rising to her knees, Aurelia pressed kisses down her husband's chest and stomach. Cristos groaned as she moved her mouth lower, his fingers threading through her hair.

Although she was exhausted, she didn't want to go to sleep on her wedding night without showing her husband pleasure.

Scooting lower on the bed, she took his cock into her hand, swirling her tongue around the crown of it. Although his thickness stretched her mouth to the limit, she still craved the taste of his skin against her tongue. She squeezed him in her hands, his length as hard as steel, and stroked him, taking him into her mouth, the salty taste hitting her tongue and making her moan. His hips bucked, trying to encourage her movements.

Working his length with her hand and her mouth, she savored him, wanting nothing more than to bring him to orgasm.

His breath sharp as he got close to climaxing, Cristos dragged her up by her shoulders until she straddled him, her own need driving her as she sunk down onto his cock. Leaning forward as their hips moved together, she gripped the back of his head, pulling him to her and kissing him, the movement of his tongue as owning as his length inside her.

When her release hit her, the shockwave of it sent tremors throughout her, the clinching of her body sending them into ecstasy together.

Chapter 36

Kason

Kason and Holera awoke the next morning at first light, the fire in their tent burned down to embers, leaving it uncomfortably cold. By the time they dressed and made it out to the main fire in the cave, Bremusa was already there, tending to the injured Norithaean. He'd made it through the night since her treatment had stopped his bleeding, however his leg was still too injured to walk, leaving him temporarily handicapped.

Before they'd gone to bed the night before, Bremusa had told them she would go out into the valley in her true form, however neither of them knew what her true form was. They knew she was an elemental, but her kind was very rare, at least from what Kason knew. He didn't know much about elementals, aside from the fact that they held immense magic, allowing them not only to shift into any creature they wanted, but to do things others in his world could not.

Although there were protective wards over the entrance to their cave, one of the fighters still stood guard, because if Warbotach happened upon them, there was no guarantee their wards would not be broken by others with the power to do so.

One of the things that unsettled Kason was that although elementals were rare, Warbotach had someone at their disposal that was strong enough to create a standing ward around the city of Flamecliff and keep it steady, which he knew was a task not many could accomplish. Even the people in his own ranks, warriors like Taryn with the ability to establish masking words, could not hold them in place for very long without the help of others with the same power. After talking with his general, he realized Uldon may not have been able to change the will of the crown with whoever's magic supported him, but he certainly had more power in his ranks than they realized.

"If the two of you can watch over him, I'm going to go out and try to test the boundaries and strength of these wards."

Setting the canteen aside she had been using to give the injured soldier water, Bremusa blew out of breath.

"Although I spent months in the same palace as the Warbotach king and his men in a disguise, I was not privy to the inner workings of his court, nor did I know all the magic he tried to use in order to bend the will of the crown. I cannot reveal everything Otera and I did in order to protect the crown. All I can say is he will not be able to accomplish what he's trying to accomplish with the crown at this point. I do know he's been looking for me, but he never knew the elemental he sought was right under his nose. What I am afraid of, from what I've seen with these wards so far, is that he may have not needed me at all. It appears as though he's found someone or something very powerful to exploit. These are the reasons why I didn't use my true form last night and I'm hesitant to use it even today."

Hanging on each of Bremusa's words, Kason leaned forward, placing his elbows on his knees as he sat on the ground near the fire.

"My true form can get me through the valley without being seen by the fae, but if he has another elemental in his grasp, or some other creature with similar powers, there's a chance they will sense me in my true from, when they couldn't have in this form, or in the animal form I took last night."

Standing, she walked around the fire, kneeling in front of Kason and Holera. Kason's breath caught in his lungs because he didn't know what she was going to do next.

Reaching out her hand, Bremusa placed her palm against his forehead.

"Whatever you do, do not come after me if I don't return. If I am captured, I need you to know where to find the most powerful object in our world."

Before Kason had a moment to object or to ask questions, magic pulsed from the elemental's palm into his head, sending images through his consciousness.

As though he were drifting on the wind, Kason watched as his near invisible form traveled through the valley, passing cave after cave, until he stopped in front of one. Although this cave didn't look any more important than all the others, the force calling him into it was undeniable. Moving forward without steps, he watched as his translucent hand rose to his neck, pulling an amulet away from his skin and placing it against the stone wall.

For a moment, all he could hear was buzzing. The sound filled his ears, creating a disorienting sensation. When the buzzing stopped, his body drifted into the cave, the darkness pulling him further through each cavern, the labyrinth confusing and overwhelming. When his body finished its journey, his arm reached forward into what looked like an empty burrow in the rock and pulled out a sparkling crown.

When the female pulled her hand away from Kason's forehead, he swayed where he sat, the release of magic making him dizzier.

"What—is it not—?"

Although he tried to speak, the words wouldn't come, at least not words that made any sense.

Reaching into her satchel, Bremusa pulled out the same amulet he'd seen around his neck in the vision and placed it in his palm.

"Do not share what you've seen, because if you do, the information could get into the wrong hands and the world as we know it could end. I'm only sharing this with you so someone other than me knows where to find it if something happens to me, and I can't get to it when I need to. With that item, the portal can be destroyed. If all else fails, it's what we will have to do to keep the barbarians out of the human world."

Placing the amulet around his neck, Kason turned to his mate, reaching out to touch her, knowing it would calm his racing heart. The information he'd been given was so much bigger than him and he didn't believe he was the right person for such a task. It wasn't that he wasn't strong or loyal, but because he didn't have the powers some of the other Ekotorians had. If it came time for the crown to be retrieved and destroyed, he knew he wouldn't be able to do it, because he didn't have the magic in his own body.

Still, he understood why Bremusa shared her secret with him. Although Holera would've been just as trustworthy for such a task, she was a target simply because she was a phoenix warrior. Bremusa needed someone who seemed, at least to the barbarians, to not be a magical threat. He may have been a good fighter, but he was certainly not anything special, at least to no one but his mate.

Still tied up in his thoughts, motion in Kason's peripheral vision caught his attention and he turned to see Bremusa shift into what she called her true form. For a moment, he couldn't look away. Where the dark-haired fae female had stood only moments before, nothing remained but a translucent swirling mass. In a matter of seconds, the entity drifted out of the cave and disappeared from sight.

Chapter 37

Aurelia

Waking the next morning at first light, Aurelia and Cristos gathered their packed bags and left their suite to eat breakfast in the kitchen. The servers had already gathered food for their journey, which had been split up among the warriors for transport. Most of the warriors would travel on foot to maintain stealth behind moving wards, however there were approximately four dozen winged warriors, both Aegrician and Norithaean, who would travel in the sky to join Kason's group in the mountains behind the city of Flamecliff. They did not know if Bremusa had managed to take down the wards, but the hope was that she had managed to weaken them enough so the others with warding powers would be able to work together to destroy the rest of the protective barrier around the city.

Pulling her cloak on and securing her bow and quiver over her back, Aurelia followed Cristos to the barracks, where they were to meet everyone else who was leaving for the journey that day. Soldiers would remain in Norithae to protect the city from invaders, but Bremusa and other warriors with powers to establish wards had put as many protections on the city as they could. Although, with Bremusa having left with Kason's group, they were not sure how long the wards would last. Because of that, several of the warriors who had warding abilities were forced to stay behind to protect the city.

By the time they made it into the war room, Septima and Exie were already there, as was Otera, Blaedia, and many other military leaders from all three kingdoms. The Diapolisian fleet had left the morning before, most of their fighters traveling north by ship, the king and his consort part of that group. The dragons under his control left as well, flying overhead to protect their ships.

Although Aurelia had fought with herself about bringing Kano to Aegricia, she ultimately decided not to leave him behind. The great tiger had been a vital part of their victory in the battle of Norithae and she couldn't deny how important it seemed for him to protect her. After spending so much of their lives together, she couldn't deny him that.

Cristos had been very vocal about the decision to bring the tiger along, arguing that Kano could provide security in the healers' camps, where Aurelia intended to remain during the duration of the war. Unlike their journey toward Norithae, however, Aurelia would not be able to walk beside Kano. With her being pregnant, Cristos and the healers insisted she travel by horseback for the extensive journey north.

Approaching Septima as everybody left the war room for the courtyard, Aurelia slipped her hand into her sister's.

"Are you ready for this? After what happened last time?"

Even if Septima was ready to go back into war, Aurelia was not, not after almost losing her sister forever.

Septima shrugged as she rubbed her thumb along Aurelia's hand.

"You know Blaedia told us from the beginning that you can never truly be ready for war. You can never truly be ready to face the possibility of your death, but we go into war anyway, because we're fighting for something worth fighting for. I know we didn't look at it that way when we first got here, not exactly. But now we both have mates. Well, you have a husband and a child on the way. I have Exie. We have a life and a family here that are everything to us. So, I guess the answer is complicated, but no, I'm not ready to die, but I am ready to die for all the things that are worth dying for here in Ekotoria."

The backs of Aurelia's eyes burned from Septima's words, the subtle reminder of everything they had to lose and everything they were fighting for. Septima may have been her younger sister, but she was wise beyond her years. Hearing Septima refer to Exie as her mate brought joy into Aurelia's heart. It was, after all, the reason they'd fled their home in the first place. Since a female was not allowed to marry another female in Vaekros, they'd fled their home to get out of arranged marriages so Exie could eventually find a female to marry and love and have a life free from the fear of persecution.

Once they arrived in the courtyard, Aurelia saw Cristos saddling her horse, and Exie standing with Kano on his leash at her side. With as large of a tiger as Kano was, a leash made of leather would not have done much to prevent him from running off if he truly wanted to, so it was more of a reminder to him of which way they wanted him to go, and it helped the others to feel safer in his presence. Although he'd grown up domesticated and would not attack someone unless he or someone he loved was being threatened, he was still a huge tiger, and could be very intimidating, so they put a leash on him, which at least offered the façade of him being in control.

Approaching Cristos and her mount, Aurelia slid her hands up her husband's back, slipping in front of him and sneaking a kiss. He grinned as he looked at her face and then hefted her up, placing her on the saddle before she even had a chance to tell him that she could've gotten on the horse herself.

"Are you going to ride up here with me?"

As soon as she asked the question, her face heated with the memory of the other times she's ridden on a horse with him. When they'd taken their trip to Diapolis and back, he'd rubbed her between her thighs relentlessly while she rode on the horse in front of him, nearly bringing her to climax many times only to tease her and let it go. She didn't know if it would've been such a good idea to have such intimate touches when surrounded by the military of three kingdoms, but it did sound like a good time.

Cristos cocked an eyebrow, his grin mischievous.

"Why, my wife, would you like me to ride on the horse with you? Would you like me to wrap my arms around you and keep you safe?"

His grin only became more wicked the warmer her cheeks got. He knew exactly what he was doing.

She shrugged, sliding her hand against the horse's silky black fur.

"I don't know. Maybe it's you who wants to ride with me because you can't handle being so far away."

He chuckled, taking a step closer to the horse until he was right against her leg and sliding his hand up the inside of her thigh.

"I do love touching you, and I don't like being too far away from you, but I will only be walking at your side. If you feel unsafe, however, I would be happy to sit behind you and wrap you in my arms to keep you safe."

When the convoy set off within the hour, Cristos sat astride the horse right behind Aurelia and she couldn't stop grinning. Although she knew he wanted to ride with her, she had little doubt that when he climbed on the horse, he said he was doing it to keep her safe. She didn't argue. She was just happy he wanted to be close to her. Although, if he did try to make her orgasm in front of everyone, she intended to push him right off the horse and onto the ground.

Since they were merely marching toward where they would make camp for the night, and not into war that day, there were no high energy speeches given to the group like Blaedia had done the morning they'd left for the battle in Norithae. The queen, however, did give some words of encouragement in the courtyard before everyone set off.

Otera spoke about the kingdom, its future, and everything that had happened and its past. She talked about the people, how important they were, and how vital it was for their kingdom to be free of barbarian rule again.

Shortly after Otera's speech, the winged warriors who were assigned to meet up with Kason and Holera's group left. Although they set off in the morning, the group would not be meeting up with Kason at the caves until nightfall. Since there was a risk of them being spotted by Warbotach if they flew too close to the coast, they had to detour further to the west.

Once they'd arrived at the caves, magically gifted warriors like Taryn, intended to join Bremusa in trying to bring the wards down. There were other warriors with the abilities to create and hold wards that traveled with the group on foot as well, so they could place wards around them when they stopped to camp at night. They would also place traveling wards around them periodically when they were in areas that didn't provide enough cover.

With the kingdom of Aegricia's capital city being warded so well, they didn't expect to see many Warbotach fighters out and about in the mountains, aside from the few that would have been patrolling their border. The situation would have been different had the Aegricians not taken back the kingdom of Norithae, but that victory had pushed Warbotach further north into the mountainous kingdom of Aegricia. So, until they got into the northern kingdom, Blaedia and Cristos didn't feel there would be a great risk to them as they traveled.

Although the leadership believed they were safe as long as they traveled through Norithae, Aurelia wasn't wholly convinced that would be the case. Just as when they'd traveled north the first time, there was a tightness in her chest, an uneasiness that made her feel as though danger was lurking. She didn't place all her trust in that sensation, however, because she didn't want to confuse anxiety for intuition, and the ominous feeling plaguing her could've been either of those two things.

Instead of traveling in her fae form, Variel moved through the pass as an enormous black wolf, prowling in and out through their ranks like a predator hunting for its next meal. She was incredibly intimidating in that form, which was exactly why she'd chosen it. Blaedia and Queen Otera led the group, Otera riding a black stallion in the front of the procession with Blaedia at her side. After all she'd suffered in the dungeon, the queen needed to rest while she could.

Traveling on much higher alert than they had when they'd gone south to Diapolis, Cristos spent much of the time watching the landscape around them for movement or attackers, instead of caressing and teasing his mate's thigh. Aurelia didn't mind because she was also distracted. After they'd been caught off guard before, she wanted to give all her attention to making sure nothing snuck up on them. Since they were unsure whether there were any enemies around, they chose to travel in relative silence, not wanting their voices to reach their enemies' ears and bring unnecessary danger to them.

By the time they got to their intended campsite in the mountain pass, most of the light was already drained from the sky, leaving them in moonlit darkness. Instead of following the pass straight north, the procession of soldiers had detoured west into the mountain valley, where they would be able to find caves to set up camp. Also, since they'd set up camp far to the west, they were not close enough to the city for Warbotach to sense them or see them, unless they'd been looking for them.

Once the perimeter of the campsite had been established, several warriors with the ability to create wards, as well as Variel, who'd been successful at warding her own property within Spectre Forest, established several layers of protection around the camp.

As soon as the cooks set up the dining tent and started roasting meat, Aurelia's stomach growled. They'd packed dried meat, bread, and cheese, as well as a little bit of fruit for the trip, but she'd eaten very little. The nausea from the pregnancy had only just started to set in, making it difficult for her to eat until later in the day. With her husband and sister marching into battle the following day, she realized the nausea had probably been from stress as much as from the pregnancy.

With exhaustion weighing on both of them, Aurelia and Cristos set up their tent and then headed to the dining area. The sooner they ate, the sooner they could shower and get to sleep. Although Aurelia knew what the morning would bring, as well as the agreement she'd made with Cristos, she still had no idea how she would handle those she loved most walking away from the camp, knowing they may never return. Part of her knew she wouldn't be able to stop herself from going after them, hence, putting herself and her baby in danger. Whether she would break her promise was the only thing on her mind as they moved across the camp in search of dinner.

Chapter 38

Taryn

Taking a wide detour around the city of Flamecliff, it took Taryn and the other winged warriors most of the day to arrive in the mountain location where Kason and his group were supposed to be. They flew low through the valley, Taryn warding them as they traveled, hoping the ward worked well enough to prevent them from being seen by their enemies. Although they didn't expect any of Uldon's fighters to be in that area, it didn't mean there were none, and she didn't want to take that chance.

After an extensive low-flying search, Taryn spotted a Norithae soldier outside a cave, emptying his bladder against the rock. She swooped down, landing just beside the male, scaring him enough that he jolted back, urinating all over his pants. He didn't speak however, since they needed to keep their voices at a minimum until they were inside the warded space of the cave. Instead of shrieking or yelling out obscenities, he dipped his chin at her and showed her into the caves that had been warded by Bremusa, making them invisible at first glance.

Walking in followed by the other warriors, Taryn saw Holera and Kason standing in front of the fire, an injured warrior asleep on a bedroll at their feet.

"How many do you have with you?" Kason asked, looking over her shoulder at the other soldiers that were filing into the cave.

Taryn turned around as well, catching Lars' eye as he walked inside with a few of his men.

"There are nearly fifty of us, so we're going to need a large place to set up camp. We did bring food. If you need more."

Leaving Kason's side, Holera approached Taryn and pulled her into a hug. She'd never been a very affectionate female, aside from her relationship with her mate, but with everything they'd gone through over the past several months, Taryn appreciated the show of affection. They'd been comrades in the Aegrician military for a long time, so they certainly cared about each other.

"Where is Bremusa?" Taryn asked, glancing around the cave, yet not seeing the elemental. "Has she been able to get through the wards yet?"

Holera shrugged.

"She left this morning in her true form to get a better look at them and see if she'd be able to weaken them, but she hasn't returned. She made us promise her that we wouldn't go looking for her, so we've just been waiting."

"That reminds me," Kayson interrupted. "Keep the warriors in the cave at night. If they must go out into the valley, tell them to only go for short periods, and not to go any further than just outside the cave entrance." Tilting his head at the injured Norithaean on the ground, Kason scratched his cheek and grimaced. "We got attacked by a wendigo last night. The beast who attacked us nearly killed him before it was put down, but there are more out there, so we don't want any of our people to be out in the valley at night if we can help it."

"And we can try to help her from here," Taryn added. "There are several warriors with me who have warding abilities. Maybe, if we all put our power together, then we can at least punch holes in the wards large enough to let soldiers through and civilians out."

Kason nodded his agreement and led the way toward the back of the cave, showing the other fighters where there were more chambers, so they could set up their tents and fires. After traveling all day, everyone was exhausted and needed to get at least a few hours of sleep before they tried to work on the wards. Removing wards took a lot of energy, and it was energy Taryn didn't have at that moment.

Knowing that within a day, the armies of four kingdoms, plus an unknown enemy, would be converging in her home for war, and that many wouldn't make it out alive, Taryn glanced at the faces of the warriors in the caverns, looking for the one who made her feel something she hadn't felt in a long time. If she was going to die in the coming days, then she wanted to feel something good first, she wanted to feel the touch of a male, wanted to feel desired. So, when she looked up at Lars again, before climbing into her tent that had been purposely set up away from everyone else's, he didn't hesitate to follow her inside.

When Lars entered Taryn's tent and saw her unlacing her tunic, his nostrils flared, and he stepped forward, pulling her against him and kissing her. They'd never spoken about taking each other to bed, had never kissed or touched, but Taryn knew they felt something for each other. They were at least sexually attracted to each other, and at that moment, that was all she needed.

Angling her head to the side, she slid her fingers into his hair, pulling him closer to her as she deepened the kiss, her tongue sliding against his to taste him. He groaned, the kiss becoming more ravenous as she tugged at the laces on his fighting leathers, trying desperately to undress him without her lips ever leaving his. His wings flared out behind him as he reached around, his top ripping as he yanked it off and tossed it to the floor. Gripping Taryn around her hips, he lifted her, her legs wrapping around his waist as he carried her across the space.

For a moment, they were only lips and tongues and limbs twisted in each other as they touched and tried to take off the remainder of each other's clothes. She may have been desperate to be touched, but it was clear he was as well.

When Lars laid her back on the bed and climbed over her, she finally pulled out of the kiss, realizing she needed to tell him the truth, even if it cost her their night together. Her conscience wouldn't have been able to rest if she'd kept her mate a secret.

"I need to tell you something."

Her voice was nothing more than a desperate pant as she searched his face in the firelight. Leaning over her, he nuzzled into her neck—kissing, licking, and sucking the sensitive flesh there, and she gasped as the hardened bulge in his pants rubbed between her thighs.

"I have a mate at home. I haven't seen him in a long time, and I don't know if I'll ever see him again, but I just wanted you to know that."

Pulling away until he could look at her eyes, Lars traced his finger down her cheek.

"Are you sure you want this?"

It only took Taryn a moment to nod. He kissed her again, his tongue finding hers and caressing it, the touch making her molten.

"If you're sure you want to be with me, even if it's only tonight, then you don't owe me an explanation."

His response surprised her, but if she were being honest, it was exactly what she'd wanted to hear. There would be no strings attached between them, and if they survived the war and something grew between them that was more than that, then they would assess their relationship then.

Confident in her decision, at least in what she needed at that moment, Taryn reached between them and gripped his hardened cock that was still straining against the inside of his leathers. Lars groaned, the sound guttural, as he ground himself against her hand.

"Take them off," she said, more of a demand than a request. Nodding as their lips found each other again in a hungry kiss, he reached down, untying his leathers as she gripped him through the fabric and shoved them down his hips. Taryn's own trousers made their way to the floor a moment later.

When Lars crawled over her again, settling himself between her thighs, he sunk his stiff cock into her all the way to the hilt as though he'd been waiting his whole life to do it and could wait no longer.

Lars' thrusts were punishing, bringing her to climax repeatedly as she stifled her screams with a blanket. When he finally met his release, they collapsed against each other, panting but still kissing each other, unable to get enough. Taryn knew they needed to sleep, but she also realized, as his cock hardened again against her leg, that it was going to be a long night, and she would regret nothing.

Chapter 39

Aurelia

Finding their way to the dining tent, there was already a line of warriors waiting to get their meal before they found rest for the night. With there being Norithaean fighters as well as Aegrician fighters, there were many more mouths to feed than what there had been in the war camp before. By the time they made it through the line and inside the tent to get their meal tray, the space was completely full.

Looking toward where they'd always sat before, Aurelia was glad to see Septima and Exie seated at one of the tables against the tent wall, Otera and Blaedia beside them. Aurelia and Cristos aimed directly toward them, sliding into two of the empty chairs.

"How was your ride here?" Septima asked Aurelia before taking a bite of her stew.

"To be honest, after what happened on our march into Norithae, how there were warriors hiding behind wards to attack us, I was basically nervous the entire time. I'm just relieved we made it here."

Aurelia surprised herself by admitting all she had at the table in front of everyone, but after all they'd gone through together, they were her family, even if they weren't blood. Septima nodded, stretching her arm across the table to touch Aurelia's hand.

"I would be lying if I said I hadn't been afraid of the same thing, especially after what happened to me last time."

All Aurelia could think as they sat at the dinner table was that her sister could be facing a much worse fate when she left to go to Aegricia and there was nothing either of them could do about it. She remained silent for the rest of the dinner, her loved ones talking around her as she dwelled on whether it was the last time she would be able to sit with them. All she wanted was more time, but it was the one thing they didn't have.

When Aurelia awoke the next morning to the sound of Cristos sheathing his sword, her chest was heavy, and her stomach was in knots. The night before, when they'd sat at dinner with the others, and then she'd returned to the tent with her husband, her heart had gone numb, too many emotions choking her for her to process. Waking and knowing that everyone was leaving her behind filled her with a panicked urgency, the promise she made to Cristos no longer her priority.

Noticing she was awake, Cristos crawled back into bed with her and pulled her into his arms. She closed her eyes as he caressed her back, the warmth of tears trickling down her cheek.

"This is not goodbye, my love. The pain from worry will consume you if you let it and I don't want you to feel that way. The future we have planned is too good for fate to take it away from us."

Although she knew he believed everything he said, she couldn't bring her own mind to accept it as truth.

"Please don't leave me behind."

With all the words tumbling through her head, those seemed like the ones that needed to come out the most.

Cristos ran his fingers through her hair, a touch to soothe her but it only broke her heart more.

"I told you when we met that I wouldn't let anything happen to you and I can't break that promise now. If I know you're safe here, that you and our child won't come to harm, my mind will be able to focus on the war. I can't protect myself if my sole focus is protecting you."

Out of everything he'd said, those words rang true. She knew if she were with him in Aegricia he would worry about her and the baby, that he would sacrifice himself to protect her. It was the last thing she wanted, but every piece of intuition inside her told her that she needed to be there. No matter how desperate the drive was for her to follow him, however, she knew she couldn't tell him, not without running the risk of him focusing on her instead of staying alive. So, even though she believed it was a lie, she nodded.

There were so many things she wanted to say, but before she could utter another word, the bell rang, signaling it was time for him to leave.

Just as they'd done before she'd left for Diapolis, she and Septima had agreed when they'd embraced the night before that she would not see her off. Neither of them wanted to feel as though it was a goodbye. So, although Aurelia wanted to spend every last second looking at her sister's face, she couldn't bring herself to leave the tent. She didn't want to say goodbye to her sister, or her friends, or her husband, so she remained in bed as Cristos kissed her one more time and left her alone with her thoughts.

The moment the flap closed behind him, the barely contained grasp on her emotions shattered, sobs pouring out of her as the strings holding her heart together finally ripped apart.

At some point, as Aurelia grieved for what could happen to those she loved, she had fallen asleep. When she woke hours later to the sound of a throat clearing, it took her a moment to realize where she was, to realize why her body felt like it couldn't go anymore. Rubbing her eyes and trying to make sense of the shadows around her, Variel stepped into view.

"I thought you'd never wake up."

Pulling herself up onto her elbows, it took Aurelia a moment to respond. As filled with agony as she was, she couldn't imagine why Variel was waiting for her to wake up. If it had been up to her, she would've preferred to sleep until the military returned.

"Variel... What's going on?"

Taking a few steps forward, the older female sat at the edge of the bed, her face more solemn than Aurelia had ever seen her.

"I know Cristos wants you to stay here where you and his heir are safe, but you and I need to be in Aegricia. You may not have a hold on your powers yet, but I know they cannot win the war without you."

Blinking rapidly, Aurelia couldn't immediately process Variel's words. Her mind was a confused mess.

"What do you mean they can't win the war without me? If I do have powers, then I don't even know how they work. I don't have enough power to make a difference in this war, so I don't understand why the war can't be won without me."

Whatever Variel thought Aurelia could do, she didn't agree.

"Aside from the power to see other people's experiences while I dream, I don't have any other special powers like some of the other warriors. I don't know how to create fire like Otera or build wards like so many others."

The side of Variel's mouth tipped up in a half smile.

"You have more power than you realize, and I will show you how to use it in time, but if we're going to catch up with the warriors before it's too late, then we need to go now. Dress warm and bring as many weapons as you can carry. I'll meet you in the breakfast tent when you're ready."

Chapter 40

Septima

Leaving the camp had been one of the most difficult things Septima had ever done in her life. She knew her sister wanted to join them, but she understood why Aurelia couldn't, and she didn't disagree with the reasoning. With Aurelia being pregnant, the best place for her was in the camp where she'd be safe. Still, Septima knew her sister, and she couldn't help but think about the agony Aurelia had probably been going through since they'd left the camp.

Walking between Exie and Cristos, Septima held the hilt of her sword tight. With her capture merely a week before, she knew the two soldiers would not allow her out of their sight, and she couldn't help but to be relieved. She knew she could fight and be a benefit to the military in the war, but she was nowhere as capable as they were.

Her self-doubt only grew as dozens of Warbotach fighters poured out from between the trees, sneaking up on them from behind masking wards just as they had done in the battle of Norithae.

Although Septima drew her weapon, Exie stepped in front of her, slashing her sword across a Warbotach fighter's chest who was just about to strike her. Blood gushed from the wound, landing on Septima's leathers as the body hit the ground.

"Thank you," Septima yelled before spinning around, nearly missing the low swipe of an enemy's blade as he rode right past her on horseback, the horse breathing fire and nearly missing one of the Norithae warriors nearby.

Running past her, Cristos' wings flapped, launching him into the air as he flew over a group of Warbotach soldiers, slicing one of the warrior's necks from his shoulders as he flew past.

The sound of buzzing filled Septima's ears, drowning out the screams and wails of war. The world spun as another Warbotach fighter darted toward her, his crimson horse lying bleeding on the ground. Septima's sword met her attacker's blade in the air, the sound of metal against metal echoing throughout the mountain pass. The skirmish lasted for what seemed like only minutes before the group of their enemies had either died or fled.

Not yet to the boundary of the wards around Flamecliff, they still had much more area to cover before they could expect to see the bulk of Warbotach's army. Still, they couldn't move forward yet, because the dead, and those who were injured, needed to be flown back to the camp west of their location.

Turning back towards the collection of warriors who were looking over the injured and dead on the ground, Septima saw her mate running toward her, her leathers covered in blood. Septima darted forward, wrapping her arms around Exie and kissing her face repeatedly.

"I'm so glad you're okay! Have you seen Cristos?"

Nodding, Exie looked over Septima's shoulder and pointed. Septima turned to look as well. Once she spun around, she saw Cristos kneeling on the ground over one of his warriors, his head lowered in his hands.

Taking Exie by the hand, Septima approached her brother-in-law, only to see that the male lying in front of him was no longer alive, but she recognized him immediately as Faidon, one of Cristos' most trusted advisors and soldiers.

Putting her hand on Cristos' shoulder, she wanted him to know she was there for him. He looked over his fallen friend for a moment, his face twisted with pain and guilt, but after a few minutes, he shook his head and stood.

"We need to get him back home so he can have a proper burial," he said to another one of his other warriors whose name Septima did not know. "Take his body back to Norithae."

The male nodded, lifting his fallen comrade, before taking to the skies on his wings. As soon as he'd flown away, Cristos turned to face them.

"We need to find Blaedia and the queen to discuss our plans moving forward. If any of those Warbotach fighters managed to slip away and go back in and inform their king where we are, then we'll lose any element of surprise we had."

Chapter 41

Aurelia

Variel and Aurelia left the camp hours after the rest of the military, so they wouldn't have been able to catch up unless the others got stopped for some reason. In order to speed up their trip, they'd taken horses from the camp, but even that wouldn't have allowed them to catch up with their people before they'd arrived at their destination.

As they rode along the pass toward the north, Variel held a masking ward around their location to keep them safe from unwanted attacks. Because Variel's wards were as secure as a stone wall, they were able to talk as they traveled without worrying about being overheard.

"What did you mean by saying they wouldn't be able to win the war without me? What powers do you think I have? Because I haven't seen any, aside from those I told you about."

Variel nodded, guiding her chestnut-colored horse closer to Aurelia.

"Since you were prophesied to be chosen by the crown and become the queen over both kingdoms, if there is no other choice but to destroy that crown, you would have the power to do it."

"How would I destroy it if it's so powerful? I don't even know how to use my own power."

"The crown will know your desires. Once it becomes yours, you'll be its master, so if you choose for it to destroy itself, it will."

The uneasy feeling in Aurelia's chest grew, her intuition telling her there was more than what Variel was saying.

"If the crown chooses the queen, how can I become its choice, its *master*, if Otera is still alive? Has it not already chosen her? Is she not its master?"

Turning her eyes to Aurelia's, Variel shook her head. "You are right in that the crown has chosen Otera to be queen, but come morning, Otera will no longer be queen and the crown will have to choose another. The crown will choose you and you need to be there to receive it, so you can destroy it."

Aurelia's heart dropped into her stomach, nausea making her breakfast rise to the back of her throat.

"Are you saying that Otera will die? That she *has* to die?"

Disbelief, followed by horror, rushed through Aurelia's body, leaving her with a feeling of dread, a feeling of something amiss inside her chest. Variel cleared her throat, leaning forward to pet her horse.

"Yes. Otera will have to sacrifice herself, but she knows this. She has for a long time."

After Variel told Aurelia that the aunt she'd only just met, who had only just escaped from a dungeon, had to die to protect the portal into the human world, Aurelia tunneled into herself, going quiet for many miles as they traveled. It broke her heart to know not only that she would lose her aunt and her aunt would lose her life, but that her aunt knew she would have to be sacrificed and had been living with that knowledge the entire time. Aurelia I couldn't imagine living with such knowledge.

As they rounded a bend in the mountain pass, the air got cooler, forcing Aurelia to pull her cloak and hood tighter around her body. The dread tightened in her chest as they moved forward and saw blood on the ground, where an attack must have happened. However, all the warriors had already left, either on their own or in the arms of one who would fly them to either see a healer, or to be buried. Bile rose in Aurelia's throat as their horses stepped through the evidence of such violence, hoping none of the blood spilled had been from someone she loved.

Chapter 42

Otera

Otera's heart pounded like a war drum as they traveled the last few miles into Aegricia under protective wards. She had little doubt Warbotach was watching the path, however none of their fighters showed themselves. Walking alongside Otera's horse, Blaedia held her sword aloft, her head on a swivel as they closed in on the location where the wards were said to have been but when they approached the boundary into the city of Flamecliff, there was barely a glimmer of a barrier keeping them out.

Wherever Bremusa and the others were, and whatever they'd done to damage the wards, it had helped. From the look on Blaedia's face, she'd been surprised by the lack of resistance in the air as well.

Making their way down the main streets of Flamecliff, it was like a ghost town. There were no businesses open and no people on the streets, not even a single Warbotach soldier was in view. A shudder ran through Otera's body, the sight of her beloved city without signs of life chilling her blood.

"Where is everyone?" she asked her mate, her voice made louder by the silence around them.

Reaching up and touching her on the leg, Blaedia shook her head. "Uldon wouldn't have evacuated the city, not when he could use the innocents as bargaining chips."

Otera clenched her teeth. Concern for her people was palpable as she imagined where they could have been, or what the barbarian king could have done to them. There was no question he was ruthless, but she couldn't imagine he'd killed them all. At least she hoped he hadn't.

The keening call of a dragon pierced the silent sky, the beast swooping low over the palace towers before flying back over the sea. Otera sat taller on her saddle as the harbor came into view, a dozen Diapolisian ships moving toward the coast as her warriors approached from the opposite side of the city. Still, there had been no sounds or movement at the palace, at least not from what she could see with the protective stone walls that encased it.

A whistle sounded only moments after the dragon disappeared in the distance and Blaedia stopped walking, holding her finger up to her mouth as she listened. The soldiers behind them halted, everyone silent as the general planned their next move.

"We're surrounded," she said, the words no more than a whisper.

Otera stiffened, her horse shifting on its feet. She'd barely had a moment to turn to look at her mate before the first of Warbotach's soldiers busted out of a masking ward, appearing as though they'd been there the entire time. As Otera pulled her sword from its sheath, Blaedia spun around, slashing her weapon at the enemy closest to her, missing as his horse stormed past and into their ranks.

Having spent so much time in the dungeon, her basic needs neglected at the barbarian king's amusement, Otera knew she wasn't physically capable of fighting as she had been before. Still, as Aegricia's queen, she couldn't expect her soldiers to risk their lives if she wasn't willing to risk her own. The queen already knew what she had to sacrifice in the end for her kingdom, and as she nudged her horse forward, it was for Aegricia that her blade swung.

Dressed in dark, fur-trimmed leathers, the scarred-face barbarians were easy to pick out in the crowd. Otera's horse bolted forward, the queen slashing her blade down on the neck of an enemy soldier who had one of her warriors cornered. As soon as the queen galloped away, the warrior shifted in a flash of fire and launched herself into the air, notching an arrow and firing it at the Warbotach fighters who had finally appeared on the palace walls.

Having lost sight of her lover, Otero's chest squeezed painfully, the worst-case scenario plaguing her mind as she turned her horse around and headed back in the other direction. Still too far away, the Diapolisian fleet had yet to make landfall, the lack of a breeze barely pushing the sails.

Screams and the clanging of swords littered the once silent air, but Otera didn't think twice about charging back into the chaos. If she would have to sacrifice herself for her kingdom, she intended to take Uldon's soldiers with her.

Chapter 43

Kason

Although Bremusa had told the rest of them not to follow her after she left, by the time the morning came and she had still not returned, the entire group knew they could no longer stay behind. They needed to find out if the wards had been taken down and they needed to know if the rest of their warriors had made it to Flamecliff. If they had, then they needed to fight.

Leaving their camp set up in case it would be needed later, the warriors left the cave for the valley, only a few remaining behind with the male who was injured. It only took a moment of conversation before the Aegrician warriors shifted and the group launched into the air, headed for the northern side of Flamecliff. With the Aegrician army attacking from the southwest, and Diapolis attacking from the east, flying in from the north would allow them to surround Warbotach on all sides.

Leaning forward on Holera's back as she flew, Kason stroked her silver feathers, hating that he was flying her into battle again.

"When this is all over, you and I are going to the cabin for a very long time."

Although his mate couldn't speak in her phoenix form, she leaned her head back, rubbing it against his leg. With the near constant need to defend their kingdom since Joneira had invaded it more than two decades prior, they had spent very little time in his cabin in the mountains and it was long overdue.

As they crossed the last mountain peak before Flamecliff and the palace came into view, Kason realized right away that whatever the elemental had done, or whatever the others who had ward powers had done, it had been successful. There was still a bit of interference as Holera swooped below the clouds, a slight film in the air, but the ward had not prevented them from entering through the boundary as Kason had expected.

Securing his bow in his hand and pulling an arrow from his quiver, Kason cycled a breath, trying to steel his nerves as he planned his shot carefully. Not expecting an attack from the north, every single Warbotach fighter was facing the opposite direction, firing their own arrows at the warriors below. The rest were on the road heading out of the city, the fight happening from the walls of the palace all the way to the mountain pass.

Taryn and the other phoenix soldiers cut over the palace toward the southwest, flying out of sight but undoubtedly landing on the street below so they could shift and fight. The Norithaean warriors, those who could fly and notch an arrow, remained in the air, Kason joining them in firing on the unsuspecting enemy.

It only took a few arrows meeting their marks before the Warbotach fighters on the battlements realized their true threat was behind them. Kason patted Holera on the side as she pitched hard to the right, narrowly avoiding an enemy arrow.

Seeing that the Norithaean warriors had the battlement and inner courtyard under control, Holera soared back toward the west, landing in an alley between two buildings. Jumping off her back quickly, Kason slung his bow over his shoulder and unsheathed his sword as his mate shifted back into her fae form.

Kason wrapped his arms around her and pulled her into a lingering kiss, wishing he could do so much more.

"If something happens to me—"

"Don't," she said, placing her finger in front of his mouth. "Don't you say goodbye to me right now."

The sound of fighting drew both their attention as Holera kissed him again.

"You promised we would go back to the cabin when this was over, and I'm going to hold you to that."

This side of Kason's mouth lifted in a grin as he laced his fingers in hers, leading her toward the chaotic scene on the streets of their beloved city.

"In that case, be careful. I love you."

Chapter 44

Aurelia

Climbing down from her horse, Variel kneeled on the ground, touching the crimson stain in the dirt.

"They can't be far now. I would say they were here within the past hour."

The healer climbed back onto her mount, urging the horse forward.

After less than an hour of walking, the clanging of swords, grunts, and screams echoed throughout the mountain pass, telling them they'd found their military at last, but the enemy had found them first. Aurelia leaned forward, preparing to send her horse into a gallop, but Variel moved toward her, grabbing her arm.

"We can't rush forward, Aurelia. You're not supposed to be here. We can't distract them, or get you killed. Just like how you move in your dreams, we will need to be not seen and not heard. We will walk amongst them under wards for as long as we can while we try to inflict damage on the enemy without them knowing we're there."

A part of Aurelia still wanted to rush forward and see her mate and sister to make sure they were okay, but she knew Variel was right. If Cristos or Septima saw her, it would be just as Cristos had said before he'd left the tent. Their attention would turn to her and her safety. It would put them in danger, which was the last thing she wanted. Although finding those she loved was a need Aurelia didn't think she could fight, she reluctantly nodded her head and sat back up in the saddle.

"So, what do we do?"

Turning to Aurelia, Variel pulled her bow off her shoulder.

"Do you know how to fight? If so, that's what you do. Pull out your bow and aim those arrows high. Kill the fighters on horses first. But whatever you do, stay near me. It's the only way to keep you in my wards and safe from being seen."

Aurelia nodded and followed Variel as the horse bolted forward, stopping just outside the cluster of fighting warriors as the city of Flamecliff came into view. Pulling her bow off her shoulder, she notched an arrow as she looked for a target. Variel moved at her side, firing an arrow that hit a Warbotach fighter, sending him tumbling off his horse before he ever saw her coming, not that he could see her at all.

In the chaotic scene of bodies, it had been impossible for Aurelia to make out who was friend and who was foe. They moved closer to the palace where the Diapolisian' ships loomed in the distance, the southern warriors not yet on land. There were no signs of their dragons, but Aurelia doubted they were far. Warbotach fighters lined the battlements, firing arrows at the warriors below. Guiding their horses around the field, Variel and Aurelia fired arrow after arrow at the barbarians on horseback, downing many and leaving their opponent speechless.

Screeching through the sky, another dragon approached the city from the west, setting fire to the ground below. Aurelia watched in horror as fighters on both sides fled its attack.

"Those aren't the dragons of Diapolis," she said as Variel's eyes followed the beast's movement in the sky.

The older female shook her head as she turned back to Aurelia, her eyes growing wide as she looked over Aurelia's shoulder.

"What? What do y—?"

Aurelia spun around in the saddle, her eyes falling on the rows of soldiers rounding the bend in the pass, soldiers in colors she hadn't yet seen. The invaders from off the continent had finally arrived.

"Joneira's returned to take this kingdom back," Variel said, the words chilling Aurelia's blood. "And I'm not going to let her do it."

Before Aurelia could process that her mother's killer was in Aegricia, Variel's horse darted forward, leaving Aurelia with no choice but to follow. She knew she couldn't fight Joneira, not in her condition, but she could kill some of the exiled queen's soldiers while under the cloak of Variel's wards.

An ear-shattering roar sounded behind them and Aurelia turned around just in time to see one of the Diapolisian dragons launch itself at the invading one, jaw clenching down on its massive black tail as they fought. Although there were warriors fighting on both sides of her, Aurelia forced her eyes forward, not wanting to get distracted by looking for her loved ones and falling out of Variel's protection.

A horn blew behind them as the Diapolisian fleet finally made landfall, their warriors a collective roar as they entered the fray. Aurelia's insides churned as her horse bolted toward the invading army. She followed behind Variel without question, but she had no idea what the healer's plan was once they got there.

The approaching army was extensive, but the numbers were not as great as the combined militaries of Norithae, Aegricia, and Diapolis. As they approached the group of invaders, their uniforms as red as a phoenix's fire, Variel unsheathed her sword, slashing it at the enemy as her horse bolted past. Variel's wolf form had always intimidated her, but she'd never suspected the female was a warrior. For a moment, Aurelia watched in disbelief at the ferociousness of the elderly female who'd taken care of them at her cottage as though she was a doting grandmother.

Afraid to lose the protection of the wards, Aurelia urged her horse forward, pulling her sword from its sheath and attacking the enemy soldiers along the outside of the lines, the others' eyes growing wide as their comrades fell at their feet due to an unseen force.

A scream pierced the air behind her as two dragons sailed in her direction, the dark green beast in front shooting the center of the enemy forces with fire as its pursuer snapped at its tail. The heat of the flames blasted against Aurelia, sending her horse into a panicked frenzy as she tried to hold on.

Although she knew she needed to follow Variel to stay under the cover of the ward making her invisible, Aurelia was forced to turn her mount around and flee away from the threats in the sky as another line of fire shot down on the enemy like a lightning bolt. Variel had disappeared into a confusing scene in her search for Joneira, as had the wards that had protected Aurelia since they'd left the camp.

Riding back toward the palace, the scene filled Aurelia with horror, causing her to retch over the side of her mount. Holding on to the saddle with everything she had, she leaned over the horse as it fled the fire, wiping her mouth on her sleeve as she heaved.

Doing her best to pull herself back upright, Aurelia scanned the sea of bodies on the ground and soldiers left standing. The remaining Warbotach soldiers had fled toward the harbor as the Diapolisian fleet and four of their dragons overwhelmed them. One of the beasts lay dead on the ground near the palace gates, although she wasn't sure if they'd been from their ally or from their enemy.

Although the barbarians fled toward the harbor, dozens of Norithaean and Diapolisian warriors ran past her, aiming for the invaders in the mountain pass. Aurelia moved out of their way as they passed, only a few of them noticing her as they headed toward their new enemy.

A guttural cry met Aurelia's ears as she looked for her family in the survivors. Turning toward the sound, it only took her a moment to notice the collection of warriors toward the walls of the palace, Exie among them.

Her heart leaped erratically as she nudged her boot into the horse's side and pulled on the reins, forcing it to move in the direction of her friend but before the animal traveled more than a few feet, a strong hand grabbed her ankle.

Chapter 45

Aurelia

Startled by the feeling of someone's hand on her ankle, Aurelia twisted to the side, yanking her foot away only to see Cristos standing beside her. Blood and dirt covered him, but she was relieved not to see any visible wounds.

"You cannot be here," he said, his features tense, a muscle flicking in his jaw. "We have to go. *Now.*"

His words sent her heart plummeting into her stomach, the realization something was gravely wrong hitting her instantly.

"No. Cristos, what aren't you telling me? Where's my sister?"

Her head twisting side to side, Aurelia looked for Septima in the devastating scene before Cristos climbed onto the horse behind her and twisted her face to him.

"My love, look at me. Septima is fine. I promise you, but I have got to get you out of here."

Shaking her head as tears trailed warmth down her face, she pulled her face away from him and tried to climb off the horse only for him to stop her. Letting out a frustrated grunt she struggled against him.

"Cristos, stop! Tell me what's wrong! What are you trying to hide from me?"

He closed his eyes for a moment as though to gather his patience. When he opened them again, his features fell, his eyes softening.

"Aurelia. Septima is fine, but Otera—"

Aurelia's heart lurched, her body collapsing against his as she sobbed into his chest. She knew what he was about to say but she still needed to hear it out loud.

"Where's Otera? Where's my aunt?"

Her words tumbled out of her mouth as broken sobs.

"Please take me to her!"

Hesitating, Cristos looked away and it was clear he wasn't sure if he should say anything more. Blowing out a deep breath, he turned back to look at her, his eyes turning glassy.

"My love, she didn't make it. She was fighting one of Uldon's fighters and she didn't survive."

He pulled her against his chest, massaging her back as she cried, the rest of the war around them fading into the distance.

"I'm so sorry, my love. I'm so sorry."

Sniffling and wiping her eyes on her sleeve, Aurelia straightened her back and looked into the eyes of her husband.

"Take me to see her."

With a nod, Cristos wrapped his arm around her and led the horse toward the gathered group, stopping a few feet away and dismounting before grabbing Aurelia by the waist and lifting her off the horse. Although she'd asked him to show her to her aunt, as they walked toward the growing gathering of Aegrician warriors, Aurelia tucked her face against his chest, too afraid of what she would see in the middle of the circle.

Looking toward the ground, she didn't see her sister approach until Septima's hand slid into hers.

"It's going to be okay, sissy."

The sound of crying, so many warriors crying, squeezed Aurelia's chest painfully, nearly bringing her to her knees as her own sobs overtook her. Her feet became leaden as she got close enough to the circle to see the locks of crimson hair spread out on the blood-soaked dirt.

Cristos held her tightly against his side, giving her the support she desperately needed. Without him and Septima, she knew she would have fallen. With her aunt lying dead on the ground, the chosen queen of Aegricia, the exiled queen's fate no longer held a place in Aurelia's mind. If Variel hadn't managed to kill her, then the other warriors would.

Another screaming sob met Aurelia's ears, the sound of someone's heart breaking in two pulling her out of her own grief as she stumbled forward, falling to her knees next to Blaedia who was draped over Otera's body.

"Warbotach are heading to the portal. They've taken some of our people hostage on the Diapolis ships. We have to stop them from trying to cross," said Kason as he darted toward them, the male dropping to his knees when he recognized his queen's body on the ground.

Exie turned to face him, sheathing her sword.

"If we let them get away, then all this was for nothing. Our beloved queen's death was for nothing. Our commander as well. So many were lost today. We have to stop them."

With her proclamation finished, Exie shifted, and before Aurelia could stop her, Septima climbed onto her lover's back with her weapons in hand. Warriors from Norithae joined the Aegrician phoenixes in the sky, along with several Diapolisian dragons and their riders, all in pursuit of the Warbotach fighters.

As Aurelia kneeled at her aunt's lifeless form, brushing her hair out of her beautiful face, a translucent swirling mass floated over Otera's body. It quivered for a moment before moving to the side and shifting into a beautiful onyx-haired female with quicksilver eyes. *Bremusa.*

For a moment, even Aurelia's tears stopped falling as she stared at the female, shock from having seen her elemental form rendering Aurelia speechless. Bremusa darted toward her, startling Aurelia back.

"We have to go now, Aurelia. I need you to come with me."

Aurelia fell on her bottom as Cristos moved in to catch her.

"Take her where, Bremusa? What's going on?"

"Otera and I had a plan for when this happened. We need to carry out that plan and we need to do it now. *Please.* We don't have time to discuss this right now. I need you to come with me."

Although she didn't know what the plan entailed, she'd heard of a plan from both Variel and Otera, so she trusted Bremusa was telling the truth, even though she didn't know the female all that well. She had been her mother's best friend after all. Nodding, Aurelia rose onto shaky legs, Cristos wrapping his arm back around her waist for support.

"Okay, where do we need to go?"

Shifting into the form of a golden phoenix, Bremusa launched herself into the sky. Cristos lifted Aurelia in his arms before flapping his wings, following the elemental.

Chapter 46

Aurelia

Flying over the palace and into the mountains beyond, Aurelia watched as the warriors in the sky attacked the Warbotach barbarians below as they tried to get to the portal aboard the stolen Diapolisian ships. The sun began to set as they turned toward the valley between two of the mountain ranges, the peaks impossibly high to travel to on foot. The rocky terrain was still covered in ice in some places and was covered in ravines waiting to swallow a person who would never be seen again.

The golden phoenix in front of them, Bremusa, let out a keening call before leveling her wings and swooping low, landing on the ground below, Cristos landing a moment later by her side.

As the dark-haired female seemed to be looking for something, Cristos still held Aurelia in his arms, kissing her on the cheek and caressing her back.

"I love you, my wife. I'm glad you're okay."

Her tears had dried as they'd flown, curiosity at what Bremusa had in store for her stealing all her attention at that moment, distracting her from the grieving she needed to do.

"What are we looking for here?" she asked Bremusa as Cristos finally set her down on shaky legs. "Can we help you look?"

Shaking her head, Bremusa ran her hand across the rock mountain face until she got to space where her hand disappeared as though the mountain had swallowed it.

"Ah, here it is. Follow me," she said as she stepped through what had at first appeared to be only a rock wall. It had been warded.

Cristos passed her a curious glance but still guided her forward with his hand against the small of her back, unsheathing his sword just in case he needed it.

As they made their way into the hidden cave, it didn't look any different than any other cave, but as they followed

Bremusa through the labyrinth of caverns and the spaces in between, she realized it was much larger than she'd expected.

"Since Otera sacrificed herself, the crown must choose another, but we already know who it will choose, because you are prophesied to become queen of both northern kingdoms. But-" she said as she slid her hand into a small space between the rock and pulled out a sparkling crown. Aurelia's breath caught in her throat.

"The crown Warbotach has is a fake?" she interrupted, her tone shocked.

Bremusa nodded, holding the crown toward its future master.

"The crown Uldon has been trying to force his will upon is indeed a fake. When I place this crown on your head, it will accept you as its master, and then you will tell it to destroy itself. Destroying the crown will destroy the portal, which is the only way to prevent Warbotach from crossing into the human lands, at least from here, and prevent this from hopefully ever happening again."

Sucking in a breath, Aurelia glanced toward her husband before turning back to Bremusa and nodding. Without another word, the elemental placed the crown delicately onto Aurelia's head.

A flash of fire erupted from Aurelia's fingers, startling her as she tried to blow the flames out before they burned her, but the truth was, the fire hadn't burned her at all.

"As a phoenix queen, Aurelia, the fire will not harm you," Bremusa said, taking the crown from Aurelia's head and placing it on her hands as Bremusa still held the other side. "Now close your eyes and command the crown to destroy itself. You are its master, so it must listen. We need to do this now."

Closing her eyes, Aurelia was unsure if it would work, but she did as Bremusa requested, repeating the command into her mind, seeing the crown in her hand. After only moments, sounds of breaking glass echoed through the cavern as the crown fractured along its center and then spiderwebbed out, the pieces getting smaller and smaller until it crumbled like dust in her hand. Before Aurelia had a chance to register what had just happened, the ground shook at their feet, sending Aurelia to her knees as parts of the cave began to crumble as well.

"We have to get out of here!" Cristos yelled as he lifted Aurelia in his arms and ran through the maze of caverns looking for the exit as Bremusa followed in his footsteps, pieces of the cave breaking off as they passed.

The quaking grew in intensity as they ran, fear of being crushed inside the cave sending Aurelia's heart into a panic. When they made it back into the valley, Cristos held her tightly against him as an explosion vibrated the entire world, forcing them to their knees. The last thing Aurelia remembered, before she went unconscious, was the flaming red wings that flared out from her back.

To be continued...

Epilogue

Variel

In the heat of battle, Variel and the Joneira were standing face-to-face, their swords slamming together, and suddenly they were caught in a vortex, the chaos taking them to a place Variel had never been before. When the Marella Portal had been destroyed off the coast of Aegricia, it had created another portal with the magic dispersed from it, a portal Variel, Joneira, and others, had been sucked into.

As she looked at the tropical scene surrounding her, Variel realized she didn't know where she was anymore, and she had no idea how she was going to get home.

THE OTHER WORLD

AN OTHER WORLD NOVEL

C. A. VARIAN

Chapter One

Elianna

"Some say the worst thing about having cancer is knowing you have cancer, but I'd say the worst thing about having cancer is throwing up my perfectly good pizza because of the meds."

A few people in the group circle nodded, voicing their agreement before Elianna continued. "My name is Elianna Foster. I'm nineteen years old and I have stage IV thyroid cancer that's invaded my lungs like Battlestar Galactica."

The entire group, twenty people sitting in a circle, called out, "Hi, Elianna" in unison, some giggling at her nerdy comment.

She bowed from the waist and sat back down, stifling a cough and securing the oxygen cannula in her nose. The one thing she didn't say out loud was that she would not get out of the disease alive. She didn't have to say it. Everyone at that meeting had some form of cancer. All their lives were on borrowed time.

"Are you going to use the key?" asked one of the younger men in the circle.

She believed his name was Liam, but she couldn't have been sure. From hearing his conversations with the others, all she knew was that he had leukemia and was sixteen years old. It wasn't often she got close to anyone from the circle of the sick. She didn't want to go through the heartbreak of losing them. Elianna's swaggering, nonchalant facade almost fractured when asked about the controversial key, but she fixed her face quickly, securing her walls back into place.

The Keys of Ecromos were the only way to open the portal in the Shrine of Solstice and cross into the realm of the fae, but keys weren't given to just anyone. For a human to cross, they had to be female, had to be dying, had to be left with little hope for their lives in the human realm. If it was a matter of survival, women who crossed over into the realm of the fae would be relieved to be there, glad even, and wouldn't fight what was expected of them. They wouldn't fight to return home. The hopelessness that was necessary to make that choice, at least for Elianna, made it an impossible decision.

According to the stories, it was rare for fae females to bear offspring, a genetic mutation that was causing the race to die out. Fae healers could cure human diseases, but the infertility among their females was something they couldn't fix. On top of this already devastating issue, most of the children born to fae couples, if the child even survived, were male.

Elianna knew little about Ecromos, aside from the rumors, but it certainly sounded like the fae needed to breed with humans before their people, and the magic they held, died out for good. She was empathetic to their plight, but she was also only nineteen years old, and had no interest in settling down and having children, even if she wouldn't have to leave her world to do it.

Aside from the rumors and legends, the portal was a mystery to the humans, as was the world beyond it. Since no one came back out, there was only speculation about what met those who entered. The door into Ecromos only allowed humans to travel in one direction. Some said the human women were used like cattle, breeding half-fae children for the wealthy, but others speculated the key given to each human woman was matched to a single fae male, their fated mate, and that he would be there for her when she crossed over.

The idea of a soulmate was a much easier idea to swallow than the worst-case scenarios that plagued Elianna's mind, but it was still a reality she wasn't yet ready for. She wasn't sure if she'd ever be ready to be a wife or a mother. The question was not whether she was ready, but whether being forced to have children with a male she didn't know was better than death.

Either way, Elianna hadn't yet decided what she would do if the time came where she would be forced to decide to leave her home or die. With the cancer in her lungs making it so hard to breathe, she knew she would have to make a choice soon. *Ready or not.*

The fae could cure her cancer and give her a near immortal lifespan, but only if she wasn't too far gone. When she reached the point where only machines could keep her alive, it would be too late. She had to decide- *soon.*

Forcing her face back into something less melancholy, Elianna cleared her throat. "I haven't decided if I'll use the key. I know it's unlikely I'll beat this thing, but we also don't really know what's through that door. And once you cross, you can't come back." She smirked, faking a confidence she didn't feel. "I don't know if I'm ready for that level of commitment. Never been much on commitment, anyway."

A few people laughed, but there were some who didn't, making her regret the joke.

She didn't know the middle-aged woman who stood, but the grimace she wore made the woman's lack of amusement clear. Elianna shriveled back inwardly, even if her face didn't give away her discomfort. "At least you have that option. Women my age have no option but to die. There are no keys being offered to us. No chance at hope. If there were, I'd gladly take it. Maybe you should think about that before scoffing at your one chance to live."

Elianna left the cancer support group feeling less than stellar. Using the key was a very personal decision. She realized that. But the woman's comments still stung, still made her feel like she was being a spoiled child. Maybe that's what she was, but she was only nineteen years old, so was she really expected to see the decision as anything more than an overwhelming burden?

Even with all the unknowns, the possibility of surviving her fate, to be healed, was alluring. Maybe the woman from her group was right, but Elianna wasn't there yet. The current treatments would not cure her, but they were holding the Grim Reaper at bay.

Tapping her hands on the steering wheel of her red sedan, she listened to the radio, willing the stranger's words out of her mind.

Elianna's mother, Elizabeth, was already setting dinner on the table by the time she arrived back home in the city of Brookwood. Her family hadn't always sat at the table to eat dinner together, but her mother insisted on it ever since Elianna's cancer had spread to her lungs. From that point on, she was made to sit at the kitchen table every night, listening to her father talk about his clients, and her mother talk about only the gods knew what. She loved her parents, but it was as boring as watching the television on static. She suffered through it anyway. Her parents would miss her when she was gone, so sitting through family dinners every night was a small price to pay. They were great parents. They loved and took care of her through it all, so she would have given them anything she could while she was still there to do so.

Her mother smiled when she walked in, her blue eyes always bright, even with the shadow of grief behind them.

"How was group?"

Shrugging, Elianna grabbed a buttered roll before plopping into a chair at the table. The woman's comments hadn't helped the nausea that always plagued her, but she was determined to eat, anyway. "Same as always. Aside from Jerry dying, the conversations don't really change."

Her mother stopped laying out food and looked up as her father, Peter, walked in and sat at the table before responding. "Is anyone planning to use a key?"

"Mom." Elianna mustered as much annoyance in her tone as she could.

It seemed the repeated conversations would continue at home as well. The way she would constantly bring up the subject of the key, it was almost as though her mother had given up hope for her. Once she used the key, her chance of staying with her family was gone. She wasn't ready to give up just yet, even if her mom seemed to be. Was ending up enslaved any better than death? She didn't have all the answers about what took place on the other side of that door, but becoming a sex slave, or only a breeding animal, were two actual possibilities. She wasn't sure if either of those was better than the alternative.

Her mother put her hands up in supplication. "Alright. I'm sorry. I just want you to think about it. Okay?"

Leaving her task, her mother sat in the chair next to her and took her by the hands. "Sweetie. You know I love you more than anything. I'm *not* giving up. But using that key would end your suffering and give you the chance at the full life you could never get here."

Just in case it was possible for Elianna to feel any worse, her mother made it happen. She never did it on purpose, but it didn't change the pressure her mother's words put on her already slouching shoulders.

"Elizabeth," her father cut in, frustration clear in his voice. "Let it drop. She has enough on her mind."

"Alright. Alright." Her mother squeezed her hands one more time before returning to the kitchen counter to grab the plates.

"It's okay, Dad. I know I need to make a decision. It's just difficult when I don't have all the facts."

Pulling his glasses off and rubbing his eyes with his hands, her father looked exhausted. "You don't have to make one right now, Firefly. The key will still be there for you later. Let's focus on getting you better for now."

She nodded, but she knew her father was only trying to pacify her. The key may have still been there for the moment, but she didn't have much longer, and she knew it. The coughing and shortness of breath were getting worse, as was the feeling of hopelessness. If she had many more years ahead of her, she didn't know if she could handle spending them as sick as she was.

Forcing down her dinner, knowing the medication would make it come up later, Elianna settled back into her role as the sick daughter, rolling with the punches so she wouldn't make her parents worry more than they already did. She may have been the one living with cancer, but they were all helpless.

The key taunted Elianna as she laid in her bed that night. The intricate skeleton key was an antique gold, enchanted with the magic of the fae and issued to her on the day her doctor confirmed the spread of her cancer into her lungs. She had laid the key there that night, right next to her television, and hadn't touched it since.

The more the air seemed to thin, and the more the pain in her chest grew, the more the key beckoned her like the call of a siren. All she would have to do was grab the key, go to the Shrine of Solstice, and place it in the lock. Then, if the stories were true, she would be brought into Ecromos and healed. She would never see her family again, never know if survival in the human realm had been possible, but the cancer would be gone.

Maybe, if the best of the rumors were true, she'd have a soulmate there, someone to share the rest of her much longer life with. Even with a new family, the thought of living through losing her parents was too much for her to bear. It was an impossible call.

Each key was said to link one fae male and one human female, making them destined for each other. Elianna wondered if that was why it seemed to light from within sometimes, as though he were touching his key and trying to get her attention. But what if she didn't like him? Wasn't attracted to him? Worst yet, what if he was cruel to her and treated her like a prisoner, like no more than a breeding mare? Those were all questions she didn't have the answers to, but they were all answers she needed if she was going to decide, if she would have to decide that leaving her world was better than staying. She laid in bed for hours thinking about it, the building pressure making the tightness in her chest even worse. Even if she died in the human realm, some fates were worse than death.

A hacking cough hit Elianna as she rested. She doubled over on the bed, her breathing becoming more ragged with the force of it. She watched the key with watering eyes, and it flickered, emanating the sudden flash of light she'd only ever seen a few times. It only lasted for a moment, but she knew it had been real and not just a trick her oxygen-starved mind was playing on her. Climbing from her bed, she grabbed the magical object, feeling the unmistakable power that surged through it and into her, the compulsion for her to use it palpable.

"You've been MIA for like three days, Elli. Where have you been?" Kiera Harris placed the back of her hand on Elianna's head, pretending to check her for fever as they sat in the university's coffee shop. Elianna took classes from home, although she realized it was a waste of time. But Kiera got to live on campus and experience all the things she would never get to experience. It would have been a lie to say it didn't affect her to miss out on the experiences so many other young people took for granted but dwelling on it wouldn't change anything except her mental health.

Elianna shrugged. "My cough got worse, so my mom insisted I stay in bed and eat awful canned soup while watching reruns. You know she'd prefer it if I never left the house. It wasn't my finest few days, but I got through two filthy novels while pretending to be studying."

Kiera laughed, taking a sip of her nonfat latte. "Elizabeth's going to find your smutty book stash one of these days and set them ablaze. Just you wait."

Rolling her eyes, Elianna tossed a straw wrapper at her friend. "Like you've got room to talk. I borrowed all those books from you."

"You're so full of it." Kiera laughed again, but her face turned serious only a moment later. "When do you guys head to Kinderside to see the new specialist?"

She'd been trying to avoid thinking about it. The new specialist would say the same thing as the last eight had. It wouldn't change anything, only remind her of the pincushion she'd become. "Tomorrow, I think. I don't even keep track anymore."

The night before any doctor's visit was stressful, even if she'd lost any hope for remission. Elianna settled into bed, pulling out one of the naughty books she kept in her side table drawer and opening it to where she'd left off. She didn't know why she bothered hiding them from her mother. Nineteen years old was technically an adult, but her parents still treated her like she was twelve, not that she minded being taken care of.

After reading for hours and fantasizing about the sexy fictional character in her current book who was totally going on her growing list of book boyfriends, she fell asleep with the paperback across her stomach.

Tightness in her chest, followed by the struggle of her lungs to take in enough air, pulled Elianna from sleep. Gasping, she reached for the buzzer her parents had installed next to her bed a few months before, pressing it repeatedly to wake them. Her heart hammered against her ribcage, every attack feeling like it would be her last battle. Thankfully, it only took seconds for her mother to dart into her bedroom, followed by her father.

"I'll call the ambulance," her father said as he ran out the room to grab his phone.

Her mother leaned over the bed, securing the oxygen cannula to her nose and reaching for her inhaler on the side table. Elianna sucked in the medicine, but the inhaler brought no relief. She continued to struggle, the air in the room inadequate, even with her oxygen tube. Spots colored her vision as the decision came to her with little thought. Looking at her mother with desperation in her eyes, Elianna reached her hand toward the metal object flickering next to the television. *"Get the key."*

Chapter Two

Elianna

The golden key in Elizabeth's hand was the only sign the first responders needed to know where to take her daughter. It was a scenario they knew well enough. With the sound of the siren piercing the late-night silence, the ambulance raced toward the Shrine nestled within the Haunted Mountains, the exit leading to the hospital fading in the distance. Grief was replaced by numbness, filling Elianna's ailing body with every mile they drove down the darkened roadway.

Elianna's parents hovered over her, holding her hands and whispering words of encouragement, but all she felt was nothing. Nothing, aside from the pain in her chest and the lack of oxygen in the air. She would never see them again. It wasn't a reality she could come to terms with, so she pushed it in the back of her mind and tried to pretend she was simply going to yet another hospital visit. That way, the fallout of her decision wouldn't hit her until it was too late for her to change her mind or take it back. By the time she would let those feelings flood back in, she would be stuck inside the realm of Ecromos, where she'd be forced to either deal with it, or she would be too preoccupied to even think about it. Either scenario would be better than letting doubt fracture her shaky resolve now that she'd finally decided.

When the key was placed in her hand, just as the ambulance approached the Shrine, the light within it flashed faster, more frantically as power surged through it and into her palm. It was as though touching it compelled her to follow through, as though someone on the other side was begging her to go to them. She felt the pull of the portal with every fiber of her being, but the hesitation she'd been suppressing grew as well.

By the time the vehicle parked, and her stretcher was rolled out onto the roughly laid pavement, the tears came out in sobs, uncertainty lacing every ragged breath.

"I've changed my m-mind. Mom?" With the pain in Elianna's chest, the words couldn't come out fast enough. "No. Let's go b-back to the hospital."

When her mother looked at her, silver lined her eyes, but she shook her head, the gesture crushing Elianna's heart. "Sweetheart. *Please.* This is the right decision for you."

Her father faltered, pulling the stretcher to a stop. "Maybe we should wait, Elizabeth. Clearly, this isn't what she wants. She shouldn't be making this decision when she's in distress."

Another round of violent coughing hit Elianna, her body betraying her when she needed it to cooperate the most. She needed her parents to have faith that she could recover and bring her to the hospital instead. She needed more time.

Wiping her eyes and setting her jaw with renewed determination, her mother yanked on the stretcher, forcing it to roll toward the Shrine again. "We have to do this now, Peter. If we wait," Her mother hesitated, sobbing, making her voice shake. "If we wait, it may be too late. You know the rules. They won't take her if she's too far gone. Even now, what if she's too sick? We have to do this now."

Elianna didn't argue out loud, her body in too much turmoil for her words to hold any water. She knew her mother was right, even if she didn't want to admit it, even if she wasn't ready to leave them. The truth was, she would never be ready.

"What's it gonna be, Elianna?" one of the first responders asked as he locked the stretcher in place.

It was her mother who answered. "She has to go. We have to do this now, while she still can." Elizabeth leaned over her daughter, cradling her cheeks between her hands. "Sweetheart. Your dad and I would do anything for you, and this is something we must do. We love you too much to let you sacrifice your life for more time with us." Elianna shook her head, tears streaming from her eyes as she glanced from her mother to her father, committing their faces to memory. "After all the years you've suffered, this is your chance to be free from the pain. This is your chance to be happy."

Her father moved closer, taking her by the hand. "Your mother's right, Firefly. It's time."

Even though her mind knew her parents were right, her heart couldn't accept what they were saying, but she nodded, or something that could've been mistaken as a nod.

The Shrine of the Solstice loomed before her, a white structure that was such a contrast to the dark mountains surrounding it. The stretcher began rolling toward the entrance again, which was infinitely left open, and up the ramp that made it easier to bring in people like her. People who couldn't walk in by themselves. *Dying people.* The white marble of the building gleamed in the firelight of the candles, making the entire interior glow with a magical aura.

Although Elianna had read all about the Shrine and had been schooled in getting to the door, she'd never been inside. She'd never even been in the parking lot. The walls were covered with mosaics of the setting sun, landscapes, and plant life, all glittering with the candlelight, all seeming to be alive.

The door, a cerulean blue, stood against the back wall, framed by large sconces, the flames bigger than the rest, as though they were enchanted. They probably were. She watched the door, watched the antique lock, waiting for it to do something. *Anything.* Hoping it would give her some sign of what she should do, what her fate would be on the other side, but it didn't. It just stood there.

Elianna's eyes darted from her parents to the first responders, the feeling of desperation growing in her once again. "Mom? I don't want to do this." Reaching for her mother's hand that gripped the railing, she pulled it to her. "Please, Mom."

The two men who brought her there looked more than uncomfortable as they watched Elianna and her parents, waiting for someone to decide. They didn't speak. Instead, they just watched over her oxygen and vital signs, waiting patiently for what would come next.

Elizabeth squeezed her daughter's hand, the key pulsing against her skin, before pulling her into a hug, but her eyes were distant. "I'm not saying goodbye, Sweetheart. But I know this is the right thing for you to do, and you know it too." Elianna's body shook with the force of her sobs, but she didn't bother arguing. She was in too much distress to make the right decision for herself anymore.

When her father leaned over her and wrapped his arms around her, her crying only got worse. "You're gonna shine in Ecromos, Firefly. Just wait and see."

She knew her father believed what he'd said, but she wasn't so sure. She wasn't sure about anything. Still, Elianna glanced her tear-stained eyes up at the first responders and nodded, feeling less confidence than she tried to force into her face. Her parents held her hands as the oxygen was removed, her lungs straining without it, but she didn't object.

"You need to turn the key, Sweetheart," her mother said, releasing her hand and nudging it toward the door as the back of her stretcher was raised into the sitting position.

350 CROWN OF THE EXILED

Without her cannula, the growing panic inside Elianna only made her breathing more erratic. She'd never felt so powerless, even when she'd received her diagnosis, even as that diagnosis had gotten worse. Her father reached behind her back, helping to lift her from the bed as the first responders supported her on weak legs. She lifted the golden key to the antique lock, her hand trembling as it aimed for the door.

Violent coughing hit her again, her chest squeezing without the extra oxygen. She doubled over as they held onto her, the key falling as though in slow motion, clanging loudly as it hit the floor.

The next moments were a blur, her oxygen starved brain processing too slow for them to make sense. She coughed against her father's chest as he cradled her on the ground, as her mother reached for the key. The surrounding scene spun, but only a moment seemed to pass between when she had dropped to the floor, and when her mother slammed the key into the lock and the door creaked open.

The room beyond the doorway was a white void. There was no way to see what was hiding behind the light, although Elianna wasn't sure if the brightness was from the state of her body, or if it was truly what she would travel into.

Placing the key back into Elianna's hand, Elizabeth kissed her daughter on the forehead, giving her a warm smile, before moving aside. Elianna stared into the void as her father and the first responders lifted her, setting her down just within the opening. The last thing she saw before the door closed, separating her from her parents, from her world, was the silver behind her father's eyes, her mother's strength shattering.

As soon as the lock clicked into place, Elianna collapsed, the light enveloping her.

Elianna wasn't sure how much time had passed since she'd been left on the inside of the doorway, inside the endless sea of white, nor was she sure if she was still alive. Snippets of visions flashed in and out of her consciousness. The feeling of hands touching her, images of people surrounding her. *Voices.* She couldn't focus on one thing. She was too weak, too exhausted. The coughing had subsided, her breathing becoming easier, but she didn't have the strength to analyze why. Maybe she was dead. A moment of panic was all she felt before oblivion consumed her once again.

The room Elianna woke in was stark, empty aside from a small bed, table, sink, and toilet. The walls were a sterile white, as were the sheets, and even the gown she was wearing. It was so void of color that it made her wonder if she was still in the spot she'd been left in when her parents had closed her into the portal. There were no windows, and no handle on the door. She was trapped, imprisoned, but too confused to panic just yet.

Chest no longer hurting, Elianna took the first deep breath she'd been allowed in over four years. Maybe she *was* dead. A whimpering sob rose in her throat, but she held it down as sounds echoed on the other side of the door. Crouching in the corner, she waited for the door to open, waited for some sign of whether she was in the other world, or if her time of being alive had ended.

"Oh, good. You're awake." An older woman walked into the room with a tray balanced in her hands. No. Not a woman. *Fae.* She had to be.

Iridescent wings, like that of a dragonfly, were tucked against her back as she turned to set the food tray on a small table near the wall. Her skin was tinged with lilac, her ears slightly pointed. Her face, aside from the color of her skin and the obsidian of her eyes, looked almost human. Even her hair, a thick black braid, fell down the center of her back like women of the human world. It made Elianna even more self-conscious about her own hair, or lack thereof, which had only just begun growing back since her chemotherapy and was barely long enough to tuck behind her ears in a chestnut pixie cut. Smoothing her hands against it, she watched her visitor.

Although the female's sweet voice, and equally sugary smile, was disarming, Elianna's heart still thrummed too quickly in her chest. She'd never needed her mother as badly as she did at that moment. "Where am I?"

Freezing for only a moment as she readied a cup of tea, the female seemed to be surprised at Elianna's question. When she turned back around with the steaming mug in her hands, the saccharine smile was still on her face. "Well, you're at Lord Argall's manor in the Court of Knowledge, Miss. My name is Hiedra. I'll be tending to you while you're here. What's your name?"

The statement made her stomach clench, the implications of it reminding her of the fears she'd harbored before using the key. "My name is Elianna..." She hesitated, scanning the room. "I thought the key would bring me to my mate, the one with the twin to my own. Where will I be going when I leave here?"

She looked around the room for her golden key but didn't see it anywhere. *They'd taken it.* An ominous feeling crawled over her, seeping into any part of her that had previously held any hope.

Hiedra shrugged and reached for the bowl of soup. "I know nothing about a mate, Miss. You came to us rather sick and it took a lot to heal you. But, as I understand it, you'll be with a new master as soon as you're all fixed up."

A master. The words hit Elianna like a bullet to the chest, her worst fears coming to life. She was a prisoner.

Acknowledgements

I want to thank my editor, Megan, of Willow Oak Author Services for putting up with my crazy editing schedule. (At least I keep the work coming).

Thank you to Charlee, of Blurbs, Baubles, and Book Covers, for putting up with me...and formatting my books beautifully...oh yea...and for this and many other covers...my maps too!

Thank you to Keni Aryani, of Babelast, for creating such beautiful character art for this series.

My final thank you is to my family, friends, and readers. Thank you for your support.! (Who am I kidding? I have like four friends.)

Also by C. A. Varian

Hazel Watson Mystery Series

Kindred Spirits: Prequel

The Sapphire Necklace

Justice for the Slain

Whispers from the Swamp

Crossroads of Death

Hazel Watson Mystery Series Box Set

Crown of the Phoenix Series

Crown of the Phoenix

Crown of the Exiled

Crown of the Prophecy (Coming Soon)

Supernatural Savior Series

Song of Death

Goddess of Death

The Other World Series

The Other World

The Other Key

Follow C. A. Varian

Sign up for C. A. Varian's newsletter to receive current updates on her new and upcoming releases, sales, and giveaways!

You can also find and follow her here:

Linktree: https://linktr.ee/cavarian

Website: https://cavarian.com/

Amazon Author Page: https://www.amazon.com/C-A-Varian/e/B09FG5YRR5/ref=dp_byline_cont_pop_ebooks_1

TikTok: @AuthorCAVarian

Instagram: @c._a._varian_author

Facebook: @C.A.VARIAN1

Twitter: @cavarianauthor

Patreon: https://www.patreon.com/cavarian

Goodreads: https://www.goodreads.com/author/show/21
810667.C_A_Varian

Bookbub: https://www.bookbub.com/profile/c-a-varian

About the Author

Raised in a small town in the heart of Louisiana's Cajun Country, C. A. Varian spent most of her childhood fishing, crabbing, and getting sunburnt at the beach. Her love of reading began very young, and she would often compete at school to read enough books to earn prizes.

Graduating with the first of her college degrees as a mother of two in her late twenties, she became a public-school teacher, which is the career she still has today. She teaches special education at a local middle school. Writing became a passion project, and she put out her first novel in 2021, and has continued to publish new novels every few months since then, not slowing down for even a minute.

Married to a retired military officer, she spent many years moving around for his career, but they now live in central Alabama, with her youngest daughter, Arianna. Her oldest daughter, Brianna, is enjoying her happily ever after with her new husband and several pups. C. A. Varian has two Shih Tzus that she considers her children. Boy, Charlie, and girl, Luna, are their mommy's shadows. She also has three cats named Ramses, Simba, and Cookie.